## Kate stared at him in astonishment

"Good heavens, Adriao! I do believe that was a joke. You should be more careful, you might actually smile at me next!"

"And think how astonished we would both be if you smiled back!" Adriao returned. He took her hand in a clasp that was surprisingly warm and comforting.
"Come along, Kate," he encouraged. "I'm sure we'll both revert to our allotted roles once we're safe. Or are you worrying about the car?"

"No," she denied slowly. "It's just been a very long day."

"For sure. A very, very long day, and I am much too tired for any more arguments. May we put aside our differences for the moment? Pretend that we are civilized?"

"For sure," she agreed tiredly, echoing his own phrase, and in the darkness, Adriao smiled.

**EMMA RICHMOND** says she's amiable, undomesticated and an incurable romantic. And, she adds, she has a very forbearing husband, three daughters and a dog of uncertain breed. They live in Kent. A great variety of jobs filled her earlier working years, and more recently she'd been secretary to the chairman of a group of companies. Now she devotes her entire day to writing, although she hasn't yet dispelled her family's illusions that she's reverting to the role of housekeeper and cook! Emma finds writing obsessive, time-consuming—and totally necessary to her well-being.

## Books by Emma Richmond

HARLEQUIN PRESENTS
1203—TAKE AWAY THE PRIDE
1230—UNWILLING HEART
1317—HEART IN HIDING
1373—A TASTE OF HEAVEN
1421—LAW OF POSSESSION

# EMMA RICHMOND

## a foolish dream

**Harlequin Books**

TORONTO • NEW YORK • LONDON
AMSTERDAM • PARIS • SYDNEY • HAMBURG
STOCKHOLM • ATHENS • TOKYO • MILAN
MADRID • WARSAW • BUDAPEST • AUCKLAND

Harlequin Presents first edition May 1992
ISBN 0-373-11461-3

Original hardcover edition published in 1991
by Mills & Boon Limited

A FOOLISH DREAM

Printed in U.S.A.

# CHAPTER ONE

Damn her! she fumed as she stormed out of the Port Office, Lisa Barham's shrill voice still ringing in her ears. Vulture! That was what she was. A blood-sucker! How dared she follow her, worm her way into the port to hurl her accusations? Ill-founded accusations at that! She'd been happy when she woke that morning, had enjoyed a nice breakfast and driven through Plymouth anticipating the start of her working holiday in Portugal. Now look at her. Not even on board the ferry and already her nerves shot to pieces.

Pushing awkwardly between two men who were blocking her way while they compounded on some serious subject, like football, she accidentally trod on somebody's foot. Turning to apologise, the words died in her throat. Her beautiful amethyst eyes wide with shock, she stared with disbelief into the haughty face of Adriao Carvalho Ferreira. Dark, almost almond-shaped eyes stared indifferently back. Thick dark hair, high cheekbones—and a nose just made for sneering down. A man she was so aware of it was frightening. A man who made her lose every ounce of control she had ever possessed. A man who viewed her with contempt, and, coming on top of the disastrous meeting with Jean Barham's daughter, it was just too much.

'What the hell are you doing here?' she demanded aggressively.

With a nasty little smile, his eyes narrowed, he said softly, 'Guess.'

5

'Don't play stupid games! I'm hot, tired, and irritable and in no mood for conundrums! What are you doing here? Apart from eavesdropping, that is!'

'It was a little difficult to do anything else when you were making so much noise,' he said smoothly. 'I should think half of Plymouth overheard you.' Folding his arms across his chest, he stared down at her for a moment before explaining quietly, his tones studiously at variance with her outraged ones, 'However, that is not why I'm here. Peter was unable to come.'

'Peter?' she exclaimed in confusion. 'Come where?'

'Here.'

Staring rather blankly at him while she mentally reviewed any stored information that might have some bearing on the case, she eventually shook her head. 'You just lost me. Why should Peter come here?'

'He did not tell you?'

'Obviously not!' she snapped crossly.

'Hmm,' he murmured thoughtfully, and didn't know how near he came to being attacked. 'Peter was to travel with me in order to comply with the rules of the race——'

'What race?'

'The Great Port Race,' he explained equably as though he was deriving a great deal of pleasure from her confusion, which he probably was. As far as she could tell, Adriao always derived a great deal of pleasure from confusing her, and hurting her.

'What Great Port Race? And what the hell has it got to do with me or Peter?'

'Peter is to be my co-driver, but, in order to qualify as a participant, he had to be escorted to Porto. He rang me yesterday to say he would be unable to get away...'

'And?' she asked ominously.

'And so I was to use you as substitute——'

'Oh, no. Oh, no, my fine friend——'

'But yes. Not to drive in the race, of course——'

'Oh, of course,' she agreed sarcastically.

'Just to comply with the rules, which state quite clearly that the co-driver, or his designated representative, must be escorted from their country of origin, and——'

'Wait a minute. Wait just a minute,' she interrupted. 'Let me get this straight. Peter is to be your co-driver, but I have to act as his representative——'

'Correct.'

'Don't interrupt! Why do I have to be his representative?'

'Because,' he drawled, a rather nasty sneer marring his autocratic features, 'a national of the country taking part, in this case England, has to be escorted to Portugal—don't ask me why—those are the rules.'

'And we must all obey the rules, mustn't we, Adriao?'

'Yes.' His eyes holding hers, he continued, oh, so smoothly. 'Peter is unable to come, and the rules state that, in order not to be penalised, he can nominate someone to take his place until such time as he can register, which must be no later than two weeks prior to the start. Clear now?'

'Like tag . . .'

'Tag I do not understand,' he dismissed haughtily, as though if it wasn't Portuguese in origin it wasn't worth bothering with. 'To continue, as you were coming out anyway, you were the obvious choice—and, before you refuse,' he went on inexorably as she opened her mouth to argue, 'take a moment to reflect what it would mean to Peter if you did so.'

Her mouth pursed, she glared at him. She didn't need a moment to reflect, she knew what it would do to Peter. Since the day she had moved back to live with her father, as a moody and introverted fifteen-year-old, into the house next door to Peter and his family, he had taken her under his wing. Over the years, through all the trials and tribulations that had beset her, he had stood her friend, and not once in all those years had he ever asked for anything in return. So how could she possibly refuse when he eventually did ask something of her? She might not like it, but she'd never refuse, and it was bitterly unfair that Adriao should now practically accuse her of being inconsiderate when he knew perfectly well that she would never knowingly let Peter down. Peter who had stood her friend when all others had deserted in droves. Peter to whom she owed so much. Peter who had not so much mentioned a wheel, let alone a race. Peter who had lied to her. Who had blithely informed her, when she asked if she was likely to run into the great Adriao Carvalho Ferreira, because if there'd been any likelihood of that, she wouldn't have come within a hundred miles of Portugal, that, no, Adriao was away. Hah! 'He said you were away!' she retorted bitterly.

'I am away,' he replied in that smooth, oh, so controlled voice that always made her long to physically attack him.

'Ha, ha. So you are here, to escort me, where?'

'My home...'

'Oh, no!'

'But yes,' he argued, his eyes steady on hers, a clear warning in their depths. 'To my home—until of course Peter can join me there.'

'I can't! I have to meet Senhor Mendoza in Porto.'

'He has been informed of the change in plan,' he told her smoothly.

'But what about the article I'm supposed to write on the delights of North Portugal?' she asked desperately. 'The reason for my going there in the first place?'

'The article can still be written. I have told you, as soon as Peter arrives, you will be free to do so.'

'And Senhor Mendoza will be free to escort me?'

'Sadly, no.'

'So I'm to travel about on my own?'

'Er—no...'

'Oh, God,' she said despairingly. 'You've been dragooned into service?'

*'Sim.'*

'Reluctantly, I'm sure.' Certainly he wouldn't have given his services willingly, she knew that; he disliked her as much as she disliked him. 'Boy, I must have been really rotten in a previous life to deserve this...'

'Not only in a previous life,' he commented nastily. 'You seem to be managing very successfully in this one too.'

'So I do,' she agreed harshly. 'One can only hope that you aren't around to complicate my next one.'

'A hope that is fervently reciprocated. Writing articles is a hobby of yours, is it?'

'You might say so, yes. Unfortunate, isn't it?'

'Yes, but more unfortunate for the skilled writer who really did need this commission...'

'How true.' I needed this commission, she wanted to shout, only of course she would never tell this man that. Not even with her dying breath. She would never tell this man anything. Ever. Especially not how much he could hurt her with his poisoned barbs. Oh, no, she would never let him see that, because he didn't think she could be hurt. He thought she was as hard and uncompromising as himself—and now, of course, he'd be convinced she was if he had indeed heard Lisa Barham's shrill voice.

'I had thought Peter more discerning,' he said aloofly. With an autocratic little dip of his head, he turned and walked away.

'Bastard,' she muttered. Her beautiful eyes full of pain and helplessness, she stared after him. Maybe she could avoid him in the bustle to disembark? Drive off without waiting for him? No, that wouldn't work, he'd just catch her up on the road. Apart from which, she thought drearily, whatever reasons Peter had for doing this to her, she owed him her loyalty. She'd thought she had his. So why in God's name hadn't he told her about this stupid race? Or about him co-driving? Presumably because he thought it would be hysterical to surprise her! Well, he'd done that all right! And why was it, she wondered with a vengeful sniff, that people always wanted you to like their friends? No matter that they didn't get on, no matter that they hated each other on sight, they insisted on the 'my friend must be your friend' mentality! Did Peter take any notice of her telling him she disliked Adriao? No, he didn't. Did he take any notice of the fact that Adriao viewed her with searing contempt? No, he did not! Yet he'd been present when they'd first met each other in his travel agency. Must have been aware that war had been silently declared.

All right, she conceded with a mental shrug, she'd been on the defensive, as usual, but it was more than justified, the way he'd looked at her with such mortifying derision. The conviction that he knew all about her, or thought he did, had been there in his eyes for all to see, so what the hell had anybody expected except antagonism? Hadn't it occurred to anyone that she would be bitterly hurt that a complete stranger could condemn her on such flimsy evidence as a trashy newspaper article? And how the devil was she to write about North Portugal with him as reluctant guide?

Hearing an impatient toot, she swung round, then pursed her lips angrily. 'All right, all right,' she muttered, 'I'm coming.' Hastily making her way back to her car, she quickly drove after the car in front as their line was waved on to board the Santander Ferry. For the next few minutes she was kept too busy to brood, but, as soon as she'd parked and made her way up from the car deck and collected her cabin number, she began all over again. Hateful, autocratic creature! Dumping her bag in her cabin, she made her way to the restaurant, and, of course, the way her luck was running, the first person she saw was Adriao. I hate you, she told him silently.

Moving slightly so that she could keep him in sight as he went to get himself some coffee, she saw him exchange a smiling word with the stewardess before sauntering away to find a seat. Oh, yes, she thought bitterly, you can ooze charm at complete strangers when it suits you! Play the Great I Am and expect everyone to bow and scrape! And they did, damn them! Well, not Kate Lassiter! she vowed. And when he discovered just how wrong he had been about her he could do the bowing and scraping!

He moved like a dancer, she thought absently, her eyes still fixed broodingly on him, his body relaxed, poised for any situation. She'd seen him move with incredible speed when the occasion demanded it. She'd seen him laughing, relaxed with his friends, and she'd seen him angry. Easy to tell when he was angry, if you knew him; he became even more polite, his soft voice softer. Like earlier, outside the Port Office. And why was it no one else ever found his cool, precise way of speaking so infuriating? Or that hint of mocking amusement that sometimes lurked in his dark eyes, as though he knew something no one else could possibly know?

When he glanced up, unerringly finding her slim figure in the crush, she turned away to join the short queue at the counter. Shuffling obediently forward, she continued to brood on her ill usage. Collecting a cup, she put it under the coffee spout and stabbed the button. Taking a milk carton and sugar she took it to the check-out girl before finding a seat as far away from Adriao as she could get.

Her face set mutinously, she stared at him. The sexiest thing on two legs, one of the girls at the agency had called him. And so he was. It wasn't that he was exceptionally handsome or particularly smart. Tall for a Portuguese, elegant, for all the casualness of his dress of black trousers and a cream shirt, the sleeves rolled tidily back, yet she guessed there wasn't a woman aboard who hadn't glanced at him at least twice, speculated about him, fantasised maybe, and if that air of cynicism that he currently wore was intended to keep people at a distance, it was succeeding admirably. Not many people would have the temerity to broach that wall he'd built around himself. Except Kate Lassiter, she thought moodily, who couldn't keep her mouth shut. A grandee of the first order, all he needed was a goatee beard and a ruff to complete the illusion. And what malign fate had decreed he should be able to get a late booking? She'd only just managed to scrape on and she'd booked weeks ago! Although she supposed it was entirely possible that Peter had booked them both on; with his new secretive behaviour, it was quite likely. That was what really hurt, Peter not telling her. A nice little holiday for you, he'd said. How the hell could she have a holiday with Adriao around?

She'd left home with such high hopes too, such anticipation. A month touring round North Portugal in order to write an article on the delights of the Douro and Minho valleys, places she had long wanted to see. A month of pleasure, of blue skies and warm winds— a month of having to put up with Adriao Ferreira. Yet she owed it to Peter to write the article, and to write it well. He had stood her friend through all the publicity, the traumas, and she couldn't let him down. Wouldn't let him down. It was important for his travel agency that they tempt tourists to the Costa Verde. Not package holidays, or the hordes that descended on Spain each summer, but discerning tourists who would enhance Portugal's reputation, not destroy it. And now she had to write it under the sneering nose of Adriao.

Feeling hurt and miserable, she gave a violent stir to her coffee. Where was the point in going over it all now? And if there hadn't been this latest contretemps with the Barham daughter to set her nerves back on edge, she'd probably have coped with Adriao. Or as well as she ever coped with him. And why couldn't her skin be as thick as everyone assumed it was? Why did it have to matter so damn much what people thought? Even here, among strangers, she felt persecuted. The armour she had so painstakingly built up shattered in a moment, making a mockery of her resolution.

When a hand touched her arm, she jumped and looked quickly round. Forcing her ragged nerves under control, she gratefully accepted the sheet of newspaper that was passed to her.

'Thank you,' she managed huskily, then used it as a shield to hide her face. To get herself back under control.

Staring blindly at the dancing newsprint and with her feelings in chaos, she forced herself to take slow, even breaths, until the writing began to resolve itself into actual words and sentences. As her tension eased, she began to read, periodically sipping her coffee. When she had devoured each and every line, including the adverts, she folded it and passed it to the woman on her right who took it with fervent gratitude.

It was ridiculous—all these people needing shields, occupation. Had the whole world become introverted? It would seem so, she thought as she observed the dedication with which everyone was so assiduously reading any material to hand. Due to an oversight, no newspapers or books had been loaded at Plymouth, and the lack of reading material had become something of a joke. Anything readable that was deliberately or inadvertently put down was immediately snatched up and devoured. The two newspapers that actually seemed to exist, presumably brought on board by people with forethought, were being passed round page by page and she glanced to her left to see if the next page was coming her way only to encounter bright dark eyes staring at her through the mirror. Hastily averting her gaze, she finished her coffee in one quick swallow and got to her feet.

Enough was enough. This was meant to be a holiday, a recharging of her batteries. A period of relaxation so that she would be able to go back revitalised to start the battle all over again. Her eyes determinedly bright, she made her way down to her cabin, but, once alone, away from prying eyes, she slumped defeatedly, her beautiful eyes flooding with tears. If they could see me now, she thought, would they have changed their minds? Those accusers who had called her hard, uncaring? No, probably not. They would only suppose that her tears were yet another weapon in her armoury, a weapon to promote her greed. Kate Lassiter, millionairess. That was what hurt, that people could so readily believe she was a little gold-digger. Was that really the impression she gave? She'd tried to explain that she didn't need Jean Barham's money for herself, but did they listen? Oh, no. She supposed she should count herself lucky that she had at least some loyal friends—no, that wasn't fair, she did count herself lucky, but it was so damned hard sometimes! The only thing that sustained her was the shock those cynics were going to get when the truth did eventually come out.

With a sad little smile, she collected her book from her holdall. Surely to God the ferry was big enough for her to be able to avoid Adriao for the next twenty-four hours? There were two restaurants, two lounges, and she was damned if she was going to hide in her cabin for the rest of the day. It would be claustrophobic enough trying to sleep in it. Staring with a jaundiced eye at the narrow bed, a bed that looked as though it belonged in a nun's chaste cell, she grimaced. Well, that was appropriate enough, wasn't it? Although if she'd been a nun, no one would presumably have accused her of being mercenary. Ah, well, she thought with an attempt at optimism as she made her way up to the deck, tomorrow was another day, and at least she'd have the long drive to herself even if she did have to follow Adriao. Time, perhaps, to get her armour back in place; time to enjoy the scenery on the long drive through Spain and into Portugal.

Tomorrow was indeed another day, a day when the gods presumably decided she hadn't suffered enough. First of all the ferry docked four hours late, and then when she eventually made her way down to the car deck it was to find Adriao already there. He was walking slowly round her silver estate car, kicking the tyres.

'What the hell do you think you're doing?' she demanded furiously.

'Checking it for roadworthiness, of course,' he answered mildly as though amazed by her question. 'Well, don't just stand there with your mouth open, Katherine; you surely didn't suppose you could avoid me forever. Unlock the doors.'

'I'll unlock them when I'm good and ready. You want something to do, go and unlock your own.'

The little smile he gave wasn't at all comforting, and a horrible suspicion began to crystalise.

'You are not coming in my car!' she exploded.

'You expect me to run behind?' he asked nicely. 'Now——'

'Excuse me,' a female voice complained with heavy patience behind her, 'but you aren't the only people trying to get to their cars.'

Turning to glare at the portly woman, she nevertheless flattened herself against the car until she'd squeezed past.

'Open the door, Katherine,' Adriao repeated quietly.

Her mouth tight, she jabbed the key into the central lock, which meant the other doors were automatically released, and slung her bag into the back as he did the same. 'Why didn't you bring your own damned car?'

'Because I did not have it with me. I flew over, so naturally I had to join the ferry as a foot passenger, and——'

'And I suppose you also managed to get a cabin!' she retorted pithily.

'Of course, although I'm well aware that it would no doubt have improved your mood wondrously had I been able to tell you that I spent the night huddled in a chair in the lounge. Sadly I am unable to do so.'

'What a pity,' she muttered, slamming her door and settling herself more comfortably in her seat, although if anyone deserved pity it was the poor unfortunate he'd probably ousted in order to get a cabin at all. Or did the ferry line keep a cabin free for the last-minute availability of VIPs? Or did the captain hand over his berth personally?

'Rather a large car for a woman to drive, isn't it?' he asked idly as he ran one hand across the dashboard.

'Is it?' she asked dismissively. She had no intention of explaining why she needed such a large car, that she had just bought it because she would need the extra space for transporting wheelchairs, pushchairs and other paraphernalia when she eventually opened up the centre that would care for the elderly and mentally and physically handicapped—which was why she'd agreed to accept Jean Barham's legacy, to help fund it. But if he wanted to believe that she deluded old ladies into leaving her their money, and that she was a wealthy parasite, then let him! If he couldn't see beyond the end of his sneering nose or disbelieve the articles written about her in the gutter Press, then that was his problem!

Thrusting her hand through her cap of short dark hair, unconsciously inviting comment, she fitted the key in the ignition.

'Why did you have all your hair cut off?' he asked disdainfully. 'If you hoped it would make you unrecognisable, it did not work; it merely makes you look like a boy.'

'So?' she asked aggressively. 'Is it any concern of yours?'

'No. So tell me instead why Peter allowed you to persuade him into letting you write the article?'

'So sure, aren't you, Adriao?' she asked bitterly as she twisted to face him. 'So sure you're always right? Well, for your information, I didn't persuade Peter, he persuaded me. He thought it would be good for me to get away from all the publicity for a while. Satisfied?'

With one of his infuriating little shrugs, he commented, 'If you hadn't blackmailed two elderly ladies into parting with their life savings there would have been no need to escape from any publicity.' Turning away from her, he asked, in what sounded like an insulting afterthought, 'Do you wish me to drive?'

'No, I do not wish you to drive!' Oh, God, how were they going to survive a fourteen-hour drive together? And if he didn't stop picking on sensitive subjects, like her hair, there was every likelihood she'd have ejected him from the car before they even got off the ferry! She knew she looked like a boy, for heaven's sake! Knew it didn't suit her! She'd bitterly regretted the impulse to have it shorn off the very moment she sat in the hairdresser's chair! She'd had beautiful hair, she thought moodily, her best feature, or so she considered, yet, in a moment of defiance, she'd marched along to the hairdressers and told them to cut it as short as they could. And, no, damn him, it did not make her unrecognisable, so she might just as well have left it long! Yet the short, elfin cut emphasised her beautiful bone-structure, made her unusual amethyst eyes look larger, luminous almost, and gave her an air of vulnerability that she would have hated had she known.

'You're being waved on,' Adriao pointed out helpfully in that smooth, polite voice that always provoked murderous tendencies.

Yanking the lever into drive, she jabbed her foot too hard on the accelerator and the car lurched forward. Grinding her teeth in frustrated temper, she dared him to speak.

He didn't say a word, but then he didn't need to; the look of superiority on his face would have made a novel.

'Left,' he instructed politely as they were waved through the passport check.

'I was going left,' she muttered irritably. She wasn't, she hadn't the faintest idea how to get out of Santander, but she was damned if she was going to ask him for directions. Taking the AA printout that she had obtained in England from the dashboard, she put it on her knee and glanced quickly down. Make for Torrelavega, it instructed helpfully. Right. All she had to do was follow the other cars that had driven off ahead of her, the majority must be going out of Santander—with obviously as much confusion as she was experiencing, she thought half an hour later. After negotiating a suicidal junction across railway tracks and turning right she then found herself with a choice of three roads, not one of which boasted a sign for Torrelavega, and all the time the tension in the car was growing, building inside her like a faulty rocket.

'Right,' he prompted quietly.

'Thank you.'

'Then left . . .'

'I'm going left, dammit!' she exploded as he inadvertently lit the blue touchpaper.

Swinging into the turning, she slammed to a violent halt as he continued evenly, 'But not in the right place. Left at the next junction, I was going to say.'

'I don't care what you were going to say! I don't ever care what you are going to say!' she practically screamed. Her hands clenched on the wheel, her breath coming in angry little jerks, she swung to face him. 'You say or do one more thing to infuriate me, and, so help me, Adriao, I'll kill you. This situation is no more to my liking than yours! I didn't stop Peter from coming! I didn't know anything about your damned silly race! I came to write an article for the sole purpose of promoting tourism! I did not expect to meet you! As far as I was aware you had nothing to do with it!'

'Then you should have made it your business to find out.'

'Oh, no, Adriao,' she denied bitterly, 'we don't all go around behind people's backs to ferret out truths and half-truths!'

'No, and if I hadn't I'd still have been blind to your real nature. Like Peter.'

'No, not like Peter, because Peter can see further than the end of his nose! Peter doesn't take other people's word as gospel!'

'Only because the English have a greater propensity for self-deception than any other race I know,' he retorted, his own temper beginning to simmer. 'He chose to take your side for no better reason than he disliked the daughter of the woman you conned.'

'He chose to take my side,' she contradicted between her teeth, 'because he knew damned well that the woman's daughter was an immoral, vindictive, little tramp! But you, you, with your so superior judgement, preferred to believe the rubbish written in the papers! Well, I don't give a damn any more what you think of me or my morals or my life! I am here to write an article! Only an article! I am not here to serve as your damned bait! Now, if you can't shut up, get out and to hell with contravening your bloody race rules!'

So angry, and hurt, and shaking so badly she could barely see where she was going, she hauled the car round in an illegal U-turn without even checking the traffic. Her vision blurred, she retraced her route until she reached the right turn-off.

They didn't speak again. Adriao sat quietly in his seat and gazed stonily through the windscreen. Kate did likewise, trying desperately to keep her tears from overflowing. If he accidentally touched her, he moved distastefully away. If she accidentally touched him, she snatched back as though burnt. Just sitting beside him was torture enough. To actually touch him, have him touch her, was more than she could bear. Stiff with resentment and tension, she drove automatically, and all the places she'd longed to see passed without notice. The beautiful Besaya Valley; the magnificent Cantabrian mountains; across the open plateau from Herrera to Palencia where she stopped to fill up with petrol.

She managed by herself, and with her limited Spanish was able to convey her needs. She also managed to get herself a cold drink from the drinks machine, and then sat quietly in the car until Adriao returned from wherever it was he had been.

'Benavente or Valladolid?' she asked coldly.

'Benavente,' he answered equally coldly.

'Fine.' That meant they would cross the border below Verin. Conjuring up a picture of the map that she had studied so assiduously in England, she mentally ticked off the towns. Chaves, and then either down to Vila Real, or across to Braga, and then the last stretch to Porto where she was booked into the Palace Hotel. And where she was going to stay, she determined. No way could she stay in his home. If this journey had shown her anything, it had shown her that. She'd been aware of him before, but not like this, not ever like this. He robbed her of rationality, of breath. Left her frightened and weak and shaking.

As they sped towards Verin and the frontier, the sun was already beginning to sink beyond the distant hills directly ahead of them. The warm, bright light poured unrelentingly through the windscreen into her eyes, dazzling her, and by the time they'd completed the formalities at the border crossing she felt as though she'd be unable to drive another yard. Spotting a little hotel tucked back from the road, she pulled in and then just sat, her head tipped back until she could summon up the energy to move.

'I'm going to freshen up,' she said bluntly. Without waiting for any comment he might, or might not, make, she walked off and with her decidedly limited Portuguese gained directions to the rather primitive ladies' room.

Staring at herself in the cracked and flyblown mirror, at the too bright eyes, the trembling mouth, she took a deep shuddering breath and made a conscious effort to calm down. Why did it matter so damned much what he thought of her? she wondered despairingly. Why couldn't she train her inner self to match the hard outer shell she'd erected? A shell that was in severe danger of cracking wide open, and, if there were anything she could wish for in the whole wide world, it would be not to have to return to the car, and Adriao. She might just as well wish for the moon. With a defeated sigh, her hands still shaking, she ran cold water into the basin and sluiced her hot face.

When she came out, she found, much to her surprise, that Adriao had ordered coffee and omelettes for them both. 'Thank you,' she said quietly, her eyes avoiding his. 'How much longer, do you think?'

'Four hours...'

'Four hours?' she exclaimed in dismay, her eyes flicking up to his, then looked hastily away. He'd looked haunted. Haunted? she wondered in confusion. With a mental shake of her head, she decided she must be mistaken. Exhaustion and tension were making her see things that weren't there. 'I didn't think it was that much further,' she added almost inaudibly.

'Not in miles, but the roads are very twisting. I had hoped to complete the journey before it got dark, but with the ferry docking late...' With a little shrug, he returned his attention to his meal.

'We could stop overnight somewhere——' she began.

'No, we could not. I have an important meeting in the morning, one I must not miss.'

With a little shrug of her own, she lapsed into silence. Staring round her, at the dusty roads, the rather dilapidated state of the few buildings around them, the obvious signs of poverty, she'd have liked to have asked him questions. But, because he was who he was, and because whatever she asked would probably be misconstrued, she didn't.

'You would like for me to drive now?'

'No,' she said bluntly. If he had asked with a semblance of friendliness, or compassion for her tiredness, she would have abandoned the wheel with pleasure. But he didn't. He asked with an aloof superiority as though he was sneering, or taunting, so she refused. 'Besides, you aren't insured to drive this, are you?'

'Probably not, my insurance presumably only covers Portuguese cars, but we aren't likely to be stopped.'

'Unless there's an accident,' she pointed out tartly.

'Ah, yes, unless there's an accident,' he agreed pithily. 'The oh, so cool British are of course much the superior drivers.'

Glancing at him, at the cold, withdrawn face, the arrogance that he wore like a cloak, she wanted to weep for the futility of it all. Getting to her feet, she walked heavily back to the car.

Once through the outskirts of Chaves, she hesitated at the crossroads.

'Braga,' he informed her briefly.

Taking the right fork, she kept her eyes very firmly to the front, her mind almost blank until the landscape began to change, grow wilder, more unpopulated. The flat, wide roads she'd become used to also changed. They narrowed until they were barely wide enough for one car, became rough cobbles. They twisted and turned, uphill, downhill, through rocky barren soil, pine forests. The scenery was spectacular, if she'd been in any mood to appreciate it, which she wasn't. 'These roads are a nightmare.'

'Yes.'

With a long sigh she twitched her shoulders uncomfortably. They ached. So did her back.

'What time is it now?'

'Seven-thirty.'

'But it can't be.' She frowned. 'It was about that when we crossed the border.'

'Portugal is one hour behind Spanish time,' he informed her briefly. 'You wish to stop?'

'No, I'm——' then broke off and dragged the wheel over as a damned great juggernaut thundered towards them. Why couldn't they use other roads? What other roads? her tired mind insisted. There weren't any other roads, or none any wider than this one. 'They ought to be banned.'

'I'm sure you're right.'

'Oh, will you stop being so tolerant?' she yelled as exhaustion and frustration spilled out in an uncontrollable flood. 'It's driving me insane.'

'You would prefer me to strangle you?'

'Yes! No! Anything would be preferable to this!' With a deep shuddering breath, she bit her lip, forcing herself back under control. 'I'm sorry. I'm tired.'

'Yes.'

'And that's why you're being so controlled. I think I'd prefer it if you shouted back.' Only he never would. He never had. Just withdrew into cold formality. 'Is that what you'd like to do, Adriao? Strangle me?' she asked curiously.

'Yes. I'm beginning to think you should be hung, drawn and quartered and your body left by the side of the road.'

'Good God. And you said it so quietly too.'

'I do not, however, feel quiet.'

'No, I know.'

Lapsing once more into silence, she concentrated on her driving. If he had liked her, if they had been friends, or even strangers, he would never have let her drive all this distance. But, because he hated her, or was indifferent to her, he didn't care. Well, neither did she, she thought defiantly, and it wasn't until Adriao grabbed the wheel that she jerked back to awareness of where she was. 'All right, I can do it,' she muttered awkwardly.

'Then do it, and kindly stay on the proper side of the road; we drive on the right here. I have no desire to become just another accident statistic.'

'Neither have I—and why can't you put up proper signposts?' she demanded pettishly as she tried to decipher a small sign half hidden by undergrowth. 'What did that say?'

'Caution, steep hill.'

'Well, where's the village sign?'

'I do not know.'

'No, and I suppose you're used to this lack of signposting and don't find it in the least remarkable,' she muttered rudely, unable to stop, unable to keep her opinions to herself. He didn't even need to say anything, she thought despairingly. Even his silences goaded her.

'Dear lord, but don't you ever stop complaining?' he asked wearily.

Yes, but not with you, she thought bleakly—and if you possessed any sort of sensitivity at all, you'd know why. 'What time is it now?'

'Eight o'clock, and to keep asking the time will not make the journey pass any faster. You're doing very well.'

She didn't feel as though she was doing very well. She felt as though she were falling apart. Dear God, let this day be over soon.

As if in answer, the sun sank lower behind them, casting long shadows on the road ahead, distorting perception, and perhaps if she hadn't been so tired, or so fraught, her reactions would have been quicker when some lunatic hurtled round the bend ahead on the wrong side of the road. And perhaps if Adriao hadn't shouted a warning that made her jump and wrench too violently at the wheel, they'd have escaped unscathed. Only she was tired, and fraught, and he did shout, so they didn't—and that was her fault too.

# CHAPTER TWO

ALL Kate was aware of at first was the ticking of cooling metal as she remained bowed over the wheel, swiftly followed by muttered swearing. At least she supposed it was swearing; Portuguese profanities hadn't been high on her list of useful phrases when she'd tried to learn the language in England.

'*Há feridos?*'

'What?' she asked shakily, finally lifting her head to find dark, dark eyes regarding her without expression. 'Oh, how the hell should I know? You know I don't speak Portuguese.'

'I asked if you were all right.'

'Yes,' she admitted grudgingly. 'And why couldn't you have said that in the first place?'

'Because I am Portuguese, and shocked, and naturally, in my own country, in moments of stress, it is the language that I speak!' Adriao bit out, formality for once abandoned.

'All right, all right,' she muttered. 'No need to go on about it.' Pushing open the door, she swung her long legs out and then got rather shakily to her feet. 'Are you all right?' she asked belatedly as he climbed awkwardly across the seat. His side of the car had taken the full brunt of the impact.

'Yes, no thanks to you.'

'Me? What the hell did I do? If you hadn't shouted at me——'

'If I hadn't shouted at you, we'd now be down at the bottom of the ravine!' he retorted angrily. 'Will the car start?'

'I don't know, do I? Ohh . . .' Leaning into the car, she turned the ignition key. A low grinding sound greeted her and she hastily switched it off again. 'No.' Pushing past him she went to look at the front of the car where it was embedded in the side of the cliff. 'Oh, hell, will you look at that?' The radiator was totally caved in and water was spreading ominously across the road. The bonnet had been pushed back into a nasty little hump. 'How far is it to the nearest garage?'

'I have no idea.'

'Nearest village?'

'Nor that either.'

'Well, you must know where we are!'

'Of course I know where we are! I am not, however, familiar with this area!'

'Now he tells me! You know I had an AA printout; why couldn't we have stuck to that? Oh, for God's sake!' she exploded when he only continued to stare at her. With a sound of exasperation in the back of her throat, she leaned into the car and retrieved her map. Opening it on the bonnet, she peered at it. 'Are we on this road here?'

'No, this one,' he argued, stabbing his finger to the side of the Geres National Park. 'What's the scale?'

Tutting again, she unfolded the map properly and hunted for the reference. 'It doesn't say . . .'

'Don't be ridiculous! It must say! They don't print maps without a scale on them!'

'Well, you bloody look!' Bundling up the map, she thrust it at him. Resting back against the car, she took a deep shuddery breath. She hadn't been injured or anything in the crash, but her knees had an alarming tendency to wobble, and she felt sick. The sun was only just visible behind her, she saw, a large red disc ready to disappear. The sky was beginning to purple and she stared about her feeling lost and unsure and twitchy. She needed action, a decision. For once in her life, someone to take charge, tell her what to do.

Becoming aware of the irritable little noises he was making, she turned to stare at him. His face was taut and strained, his thick dark hair ruffled untidily across his forehead, and she didn't want him to hate her any more; she wanted him to smile at her, give comfort. Such a fool as you are, Kate. Her eyes wide and shiny with unshed tears, she swallowed hard before attempting to speak.

'Did you find one?'

'No,' he denied flatly as he spread the map out again.

He had long slim hands, she noticed, elegant, the nails well cared for, sensitive hands, and if he had liked her, he would have held her, comforted her— then she hastily blocked out her thoughts before she did something totally stupid, like beg. 'It will be dark soon,' she murmured for no particular reason other than that it filled the silence.

'I know.'

'Perhaps another car will come along.'

'Perhaps.'

'So, in the meantime,' she persevered, her voice raspy and uneven, hurting, 'what do we do? Try to fix the car?'

'You have a spare radiator, do you?' With a look of disgust, he bundled the map up and thrust it into her car. Turning on his heel, he walked round to the front and yanked up the crumpled bonnet.

'What else is wrong with it?' she asked as she came to stand beside him.

'How the hell should I know?' With one elegant finger, he fastidiously lifted a loose wire and looked down his nose at it.

'Well, what's that?'

'A wire?'

'Oh, funnee. What does it do?'

'I haven't the remotest idea.'

'Don't play silly games!' she yelled, her voice on the edge of hysteria. 'You must know what it does. All men know about cars!'

'Well, this one doesn't,' he refuted stonily. 'I don't know an oil filter from a sparking plug!'

'Of course you do! Even I know that!'

'Then you mend it!' he shouted. Standing back, he made a sarcastically eloquent gesture with one arm.

'Well, if it was the oil filter or the sparking plug I would! Only it isn't, is it?'

'How should I know? I just finished telling you I don't know anything about cars!'

'Oh, terrific! I have the whole of the male population to choose from and I end up with a Portuguese yuppie!'

'My sincere apologies, Miss Lassiter!' he gritted, his eyes blazing. 'Had I known of this contingency I would naturally have taken a car maintenance course!' Elbowing her to one side, he peered back into the engine.

'Like a pig looking into a watch,' she muttered disparagingly.

'So what does that make you?' he swung round to demand.

Staring at him, at that haughty, arrogant face, she spun away, her vision blurred. Oh, God. Taking a deep, ragged breath, she made a determined effort to calm down, then turned back. 'A piggess?' she offered, her tone conciliatory.

As he gazed back at her, his anger quite suddenly drained away and his shoulders slumped tiredly. 'I can think of other things to call you,' he muttered as he slammed down the bonnet. 'Well, now that we've discovered our mutual ignorance of mechanical devices, what do you suggest we do next?'

'Walk?' she asked unhappily.

'Ah, yes, I was afraid you'd say that.' Staring down at his highly polished black shoes, he gave a defeated sigh. 'You British do have a love of walking, don't you?'

'Don't the Portuguese?'

'No, we are much more sensible. Do you have warning triangles?'

'Yes.'

'Then we had best set them out, hadn't we?'

When they'd been prominently displayed, and Adriao had wiped his hands on his once snowy white handkerchief, she collected her bag and sweater. Handing him his holdall, she gave a sad last look at her car.

'Will it be all right? It sticks out quite a long way.'

'If you are expecting me to bodily lift it closer to the cliff-face, Miss Lassiter, you have a higher judgement of my powers than I do. And why you had to have such a large car in the first place, defeats me!'

'Well, it would, wouldn't it?' she asked tiredly. 'Because you never bothered to find out anything about me for yourself. Just relied on other people's opinions.'

'So why do you?'

'So that I can stack up the bodies of wealthy old ladies I'm attempting to blackmail,' she retorted facetiously. Oh, why bother? she wondered drearily; even if she told him, he wouldn't believe her. He hadn't believed Peter. Slinging her bag on to her shoulder, she began walking down the road.

'Will the luggage be all right?' she asked as he came alongside her.

'You expect me to carry your two suitcases, a holdall and my own bag?' he asked with soft sarcasm.

'No. I merely asked if it would be all right,' she retorted stiffly. 'It doesn't matter.'

'No, of course it doesn't. The wealthy Kate Lassiter can easily afford to replace anything that's lost.'

Coming to an abrupt halt, she closed her eyes in defeat. 'Dear lord, but you just can't leave it alone, can you?' she asked tearfully. 'I've been driving solidly for nigh on twelve hours. I've been forced into a cliff-face by a suicidal maniac. And now, now, when I'm tired, upset and aching, you have to start all over again.' Her eyes prickling, she swung away and began to hurry down the road ahead of him. Furious with herself for being so upset, furious with him, she didn't watch where she was going. Stepping on a loose stone, she felt her ankle twisted from under her and with a cry of surprise she fell over the edge of the road.

'Kate!'

Too busy trying to halt her downward progress to answer as she slithered down the dry, crumbling slope, she finally fetched up in a crumpled heap at the bottom.

'Kate!'

'What?' she muttered bitterly, hardly loud enough for him to hear. Of all the damned fool things to do! She wanted to lay her head on her arms and sob.

Hearing his muttered imprecations, she turned her head to watch him slither less than gracefully down to join her.

'Are you injured?'

'No,' she said stonily.

'Only your dignity, hmm?' he queried, and, unexpectedly, his voice held an edge of compassion. 'Don't you ever look where you're going?'

'Obviously not.'

Feeling an absolute idiot, she brushed herself down. Why, why, why, she demanded of herself, why couldn't she be cool, calm, rational when she was with him? Why did she always have to do such stupid things in his presence?

Retrieving her sweater, she slung it round her shoulders and faced him defiantly, daring him to say anything further.

Returning her glare, he suddenly gave a twisted smile. 'Are you always this aggressive,' he asked quietly, 'or is it only me?'

'What did you expect, Adriao? That I would accept your insults with a smile?' Looking away from him, at the bleak, barren landscape, she gave a long sigh. 'No, not only you,' she admitted honestly. Although, in truth, she was never this bad with anyone else; didn't so over-react just to being looked at. 'Shall we go?' she asked wearily.

'For sure.' He sounded as exhausted and fed up as she did.

Staring up towards the road, a very long way up towards the road, she suddenly realised, she gave a despairing sigh. It was almost completely dark now and she really didn't think she had the energy to emulate a mountain goat. 'How on earth are we going to get back up there?'

'I don't think we are,' he denied slowly. Staring round him in the failing light, he suddenly pointed across the rough and bumpy ground before them. 'If we walk across there, towards where the road dips down, it won't be so far to climb up. Yes?'

'All right. Pity we don't have a torch. Oh, well, standing here won't accomplish anything, will it?' Hoisting her bag more comfortably on to her shoulder, making a determined effort at normality, she glanced at him. 'Lead on, then.'

With a little nod, he set off across the open ground, Kate beside him. 'Do try not to fall down any holes,' he commanded softly.

'I'll do my best,' she said stiffly. Turning her head away from him, she stared round her. She could see water glinting in the distance and hoped it wasn't a river they'd have to negotiate, although, if it was, no doubt the competent Adriao Carvalho Ferreira would knock them up a raft, she thought sourly.

As the moon sailed into view throwing silvery shadows, she glanced down to where she was putting her feet. With the way her luck was going, she *would* fall down a hole, a twenty-foot one. And, the way her companion felt about her, he'd probably leave her there.

At first, the going was relatively easy, the ground rocky but flat, but after they'd been walking for about half an hour it began to change, break up into gulleys and scrubby grass, and Kate began to lag behind.

'You are all right?' he asked, halting and waiting for her to catch up.

'Oh, sure. Stumbling around in the dark is my absolute idea of heaven.'

'You think it is mine?'

'Oh, don't start that all again!' she reproved irritably. 'I'm hot, tired, my feet ache, and I'm thirsty. And I wasn't complaining,' she added quickly just in case she was about to get another lecture, 'merely stating facts. And if you dare to tell me it's my own fault I'll hit you.'

'Well, certainly the threat of that will ensure my timidity,' he agreed smoothly.

Halting abruptly, she stared at him in astonishment. 'Good heavens, Adriao! I do believe that was a joke. You want to be careful, you might actually smile at me next!'

'And think how astonished we would both be if you smiled back!' he returned, and, with something that might just have been a smile, he took her hand in a clasp that was surprisingly warm and comforting. 'Come along, Kate,' he encouraged, as he began helping her over the rocky ground. 'And I wouldn't worry about it, I'm sure we'll both revert to our allotted roles once we are safe. Or are you still worrying about the car?'

'No,' she denied slowly. In truth she'd forgotten all about the car; her mind had been more taken up with Adriao's peculiar behaviour. And it was peculiar. Since the first time they'd met, they'd been spitting at each other like angry snakes, and she was having a little trouble reconciling herself to this new Adriao who actually made jokes. Not that she didn't think he made jokes with other people, it was the making jokes with her that was so confusing. 'No,' she denied again. 'It just seems to have been a very long day.'

'For sure. A very, very long day, and I am much too tired for any more arguments.'

Oh, well, she thought, that solved the riddle of the joke, and wondered why the thought depressed her.

She wanted to snatch her hand away from the warm comfort of his, and she wanted it to stay, wanted to be held in his strong arms and comforted.

'May we not put aside our differences for the moment?' he asked gently. 'Pretend we are at least civilised?'

'For sure,' she agreed tiredly, echoing his own phrase, one that he seemed to use quite often, and he smiled, his teeth gleaming whitely in the darkness.

Echoing his smile, albeit a trifle sadly, she suddenly froze, the hairs on the back of her neck prickling as a long drawn out howl rent the still air. 'What the hell was that?' she asked shakily.

'Only a wolf.'

'Only a...' Peering up at him, seeing no sign of amusement, she exclaimed in shock, 'You aren't joking, are you?'

'No, of course not. There are wolves, wild cats, deer, even the golden eagle... They won't hurt you, you know. Even if they ventured out of the park, which I don't think they do, they wouldn't come near us. They only sound so close because it is a still night. And I don't believe for a moment that the intrepid Kate Lassiter is afraid.'

'Don't you? Then you should,' she retorted, moving closer to him and looking rather worriedly over her shoulder. 'There's something rather primeval about a wolf's howl and I don't mind admitting that it makes the hair on the back of my neck prickle.'

'You are really worried?' he asked softly, turning to face her and placing gentle hands on her shoulders.

'Yes. No. Oh, how the hell should I know?' she mumbled. 'I expect it's just exhaustion making me nervous.'

'Which hasn't been helped by my behaviour,' he admitted unexpectedly.

Amazed all over again, she stared at him stupidly, and for once in her life was completely robbed of words.

'I am sorry, Katherine,' he continued, 'I do not have the right to censure you.'

'No,' she agreed a trifle bleakly. But then neither had anyone else, and that didn't stop them, did it? Thoroughly confused by the change in him, but for some odd, nebulous reason not wanting him to see any weakness in her, she said hastily, 'We'd better get on.'

'Yes,' he agreed, and, oddly, he sounded almost as despondent as she felt.

'Funny we haven't seen another car, isn't it?' she said awkwardly, still knocked off balance by his unexpected gentleness, the flare of warmth that had flowed briefly between them.

'Well, I don't know about funny,' he commented drily. 'In my opinion, it's extremely inconvenient.'

'That isn't what I meant,' she denied with a small smile. 'As you very well know. You have a perfect command of English, even colloquial——'

'Which is more than can be said of your Portuguese.'

'Yes. Terrible, isn't it, how we always expect foreigners to learn our language? But I did try,' she insisted, knowing she sounded stilted, but unable to do anything about it. 'I got a language tape from the library, only I had awful trouble distinguishing between the "ssh"'s and the "zz"'s. I can say a few things, but only when I'm not scrambled up.'

'And do you often get scrambled up?' he asked softly.

'Yes,' she admitted, 'I'm rather afraid I do.'

'Especially with men?'

Giving him a sharp look, she suddenly shrugged. What the hell did it matter? 'Yes,' she agreed, 'especially with men.'

'Why?' he probed almost gently.

'I don't know,' she sighed. 'My mother always said it was a lack of grace, an inability to handle compliments. Personally, I think it has something to do with the fact that she had so many of them—men, I mean—that I got confused.'

'She divorced your father when you were quite young, didn't she?'

'Mmm, when I was five. I'd just get used to one "uncle" when he was replaced by someone else, and so on until I was fifteen when she died and I went to live with my father.'

'And?'

'And I didn't get on with him either,' she admitted with a bitter little laugh. 'Me, I don't get on with anyone.'

'Except elderly ladies,' he put in softly.

'Yes. And elderly men.'

'Of course, let us not forget the elderly men,' he agreed with a small smile that she didn't see, his expression for once gentle when he looked at her. 'So now tell me how it is that you are to write this article? No, don't bite my head off,' he added hastily, as she stiffened and came to another halt. 'I ask only out of curiosity, truly. It will pass the time more quickly if we talk.'

Mollified, she began walking again. Thinking back to how it had all begun, she gave a small smile. 'Peter has known me since I moved back with my father. He lived next door, and always rather treated me as though I were his kid sister. To advise, sort out,' she admitted with a little grimace. 'When my father died, I sort of drifted, didn't know what to do with myself, and Peter, who's firmly of the opinion that the Devil makes work for idle hands, decided I should do something constructive. The only thing I was marginally any good at at school was English, so he persuaded me to try my hand at article writing, and, seeing as he was in the travel business, I wrote about travel. A couple of articles I wrote on Italy and France were actually published in a travel guide. So, when he embarked on his scheme for concentrating on North Portugal, and he told me about your tourist board's desire to attract more people to the Costa Verde, and, as you very well know, I wanted to get away for a while to escape the publicity, it seemed a good idea to kill two birds with one stone.' Stealing a glance up at his face, which was set in rather thoughtful lines, she asked, with her customary stiffness, 'Are you afraid I'll write a damaging article?'

'Damaging? No. The truth of the matter is that I didn't want it written at all. I was overruled by the board. Oh, I know all the arguments for and against, that tourism will promote wealth, but wealth for whom? Foreign property developers? Travel agents? Will it promote wealth for our own people?'

'Well, it will for restaurants, hotels,' she explained with a slight frown.

'And who owns those hotels? Those restaurants?'

'Not the Portuguese?' she asked, surprised.

'No, not the Portuguese.'

'Oh. Yet surely in the villages, the little towns, even Porto and Lisbon, hotels must be owned by the locals.'

'Of course. Now. But to promote tourism, to encourage people to stay, those hotels will need to be

modernised, brought up to a certain standard, and
how do you suppose these locals could afford to do
so? No, Katherine, big consortiums buy them up and
we will end up with lager louts, tacky gift shops, mock
English pubs...'

'Not necessarily,' she argued. 'Not if it's done
properly. If you can keep it exclusive, small hotels,
good restaurants, avoid the mistakes Spain has
made——'

'Oh, I know all this,' he said wearily. 'We have
argued it back and forth for years, and tourism on a
larger scale will come, is already starting, and we are
trying to push laws through that forbid the foreign
investor from interfering, but it is not easy. The
thought of money makes people greedy.'

'Which is understandable when there is so much
poverty,' she argued defensively. 'And if that was
another little dig at me—— '

'It wasn't,' he denied mildly. 'Stop being so
defensive, and do you honestly think the poverty will
disappear when hordes of tourists come rampaging
through my lovely country? Coach tours? Package
flights? And, even if it does, will that make up for
having our women molested? Our youth made dis-
satisfied by the wealth of others? Tourism will come,
I know that, I am not a fool, but we need to encourage the best, not the worst.'

'And you think any article that the dreaded Kate
Lassiter would write would automatically encourage
the worst?' she demanded.

'I do not know; how could I? I have not seen any
of your articles. I merely meant that I think an article
of any sort is premature. We have tourists now, discerning ones, older ones perhaps, and no more than
I do they wish to see it spoiled. Is it selfish to want

your country to stay as it is? We have problems, I know we do, but slowly it is changing, becoming better. Since the revolution——'

'The revolution?' she asked in astonishment. 'What revolution?'

'In 1974. A bloodless one,' he added with another small smile. 'Since Mário Soares became President of the Republic and Cavaco Silva is Prime Minister, many changes have taken place. Education is better, more schools, our universities are now some of the finest in the world. There is more enterprise, better wages— not as good as they should be yet, but changing. It is a slow process, but we are doing it, ourselves.' Turning to her, his face more impassioned than she had ever seen it, he continued, 'You think I have not seen the troubles they have on the Costa Brava? The nightclubs, the "Tea that Mother Makes" shops? I do not want that for here! Even in the Algarve they are admitting to their mistakes, mistakes we must not make! Even in London I have seen tacky tourist shops, the exploitation of tourism! I love my country, Katherine! I do not want it damaged!'

'I don't want it damaged either,' she said quietly, her stiffness forgotten. Putting a hand on his arm to halt him for a moment, she added sincerely, 'I merely want to give a feel of the country, a view of the people, as they are. Show them the Douro and Minho Valleys, your national parks, your mountains. And lager louts don't wish to look at mountains, now, do they? Apart from which, it's not exactly easily accessible, is it?' she asked wryly as she indicated the barren landscape, the narrow road, which thankfully was now clearly visible. 'And although I don't personally know any lager louts, I can't quite see them roaming round here!'

'True,' he agreed wryly. 'I even begin to think a lager lout might be most welcome.'

'Yes.' Aware that her hand was still lying on his arm, she removed it with a jerky little movement. 'Is that why you were so angry when we met? Not because it was me, but because you didn't want the article written?'

'Partly,' he admitted. But he didn't explain what else it had been.

Presumptuous, she supposed, to think that it might have been because of her. He probably didn't give her a thought from one minute to the next. Needing to change the subject, dispel the tension that had formed again, the awareness that she had managed to forget for a while, she asked quietly, 'Is this still the Serra de Barroso?'

With a dry little laugh, he shrugged. 'I have not the remotest idea, only that we are in a mountain range and that the Geres National Park forms part of it. Loath as I am to admit it, I am not entirely familiar with the far north. I have lived most of my life either in Lisbon or near Porto, and, apart from the odd drive in the immediate vicinity of my home, I am ashamed to admit, I know very little about it.'

'Oh. So it isn't much good my asking you if that stretch of water is a river, is it?'

'Now, that I do know! It is a man-made lake, for water sports, trout fishing. There is, I believe, a *pousada*—you know what a *pousada* is?'

'Yes,' she agreed with a smile, 'they are inns, often in converted castles, monasteries, forts. I also know that they are spread the length and breadth of Portugal and that usually you can only stay for up to three nights.'

'Very good. There is one not far from here where they organise hunting, shooting, fishing, mountaineering. It is the how far from here that is bothering me. I think, and only think, mind you, that it is at Canicaday——' Breaking off, he tilted his head in a listening attitude. 'I hear a car.'

Staring intently ahead, she suddenly saw a flash of light on the road ahead of them. 'It's going the wrong way——' she began.

'*Não importante*. It doesn't matter, he will be able to tell us how far to the village——'

'You go—go on, you can move faster than me! Hurry up, else he will have passed!'

Not one to waste time in argument, he gave a little nod and broke into a run. Following as fast as she could, her eyes riveted on his running figure, she gave a yell of disgust as her foot sank up to the ankle in water. 'Oh, hell.' Removing her foot with a squelching sound, she shook it irritably before skirting the marshy ground at the edge of the lake. Hurrying on again, she reached the short incline up to the road where Adriao had obviously managed to stop the truck.

Clasping the hand he reached down to her, she hauled herself up to the road, then grimaced as she saw the state of the vehicle. The engine sounded as though it was on its last legs, and acrid blue smoke was spurting arthritically from its exhaust. The driver was old and withered, a tattered old cap perched on his head, and, as Kate appeared, he grinned widely at her.

'He will take us as far as my home—for a small remuneration,' Adriao added somewhat tartly as the door was thrown open for them to climb in.

Did he expect the man to do it for love? Kate wondered. Because he was important? She didn't want him to be like that, she found, didn't want...

'What's wrong?' he asked as she continued to hesitate.

'Nothing,' she denied hastily. Shaking her head as if to emphasise it, she looked into the cab. A goat was scrunched up under the dashboard, its devil's eyes fixed unblinkingly on them. When the driver said something and roared with laughter, Adriao turned to explain, a look of long suffering on his face.

'Do not, on any account, kick the goat. I am informed, reliably I am sure, that it bites.'

'Oh, God. How far is it to your home?'

'Normally, one half-hour. In this? If it survives the journey at all? Who knows? But seeing as the choices are limited, in you go.'

Climbing in, she smiled at the driver, offering a hesitant, *'Boa noite.'*

*'Boa noite, senhora,'* he replied formally, as though she were climbing into some immaculate limousine instead of a smelly old truck. And, boy, did it smell. The goat, she supposed.

'Is it his pet?' she whispered as Adriao climbed in beside her.

'I didn't like to ask,' he said, wrinkling his nose fastidiously. 'Can you move up further? I can't get my feet in.'

Hunching up as far as she could until all three were squashed together, she grabbed the dashboard to prevent herself being flung on top of the goat, who had decided her knee was a very good place to put his head, as the elderly driver proceeded to execute a fourteen-point turn on the narrow road.

'Tell it to get off!' she spat.

'You tell it. I have no desire to have my fingers chewed.'

'Coward!'

'Quite right, and would you please take your elbow out of my—er—groin.'

With a wary eye on the goat, she sat as still as possible, her breath held to avoid inhaling goat aroma, and to avoid any further unnecessary contact with Adriao. She was already far too conscious of the warmth of his body pressed to her side, his soft breath against her cheek as he was forced to sit sideways in order to close the door. He felt solid, and masculine, and it would be so nice to relax, curve against him, put her head on his shoulder. Unhappily aware of the reaction she was likely to get should she do so, she remained uncomfortably stiff; anyway, she didn't think she was quite ready to admit that she might have misjudged him, that he wasn't entirely the arrogant and cynical man she had thought, uncaring of anyone's opinions but his own. If he could care so passionately about his country, he couldn't be all bad, could he?

# CHAPTER THREE

HER attention riveted on the goat, Kate didn't take much notice of where they were going and was surprised when the truck ground to a halt in what seemed like the middle of nowhere.

Much too weary to ask questions, she merely gave the driver a tired smile and allowed Adriao to help her out. As the truck turned and croaked away, she let Adriao to take her hand and lead her up a steep incline. A rather long way up a steep incline.

'Oh, my God, don't tell me you live on top of a mountain?'

'*Sim*, Kate. I'm rather afraid I do. Not much further, I promise. See up there?'

Lifting her head, she stared in bewilderment at what looked like a castle—Dracula's castle, even up to the pointed towers at each end and the crenellated battlements. 'And there's me without my garlic,' she muttered tiredly.

'Garlic?' he queried in confusion.

'Dracula, you know—oh, never mind.'

Concentrating on where she was putting her feet, bent almost double on the steep slope, she obediently climbed the front steps and accompanied him into a dark entryway.

'Everyone will be asleep,' he said quietly. 'I would wish not to wake them if we can help it. You can manage in the dark?'

'Yes, of course.'

With his hand on her elbow, she accompanied him up stone stairs to a wide landing and then along to an ornate wooden door that he quietly opened. Moving inside, he put on a small side lamp.

'The bathroom is through that door. There should be everything you need; the room is always kept ready for unexpected guests. You wish anything? Coffee? Tea?'

'No, thank you, Adriao. I'm much too tired.'

'All right, sleep well, Katherine, I'll see you in the morning. And Kate,' he added, turning back to her, 'I am sorry for my behaviour.' As she stared at him in astonishment, he raised one eyebrow in query as though he couldn't in the least understand her surprise. 'You think I enjoyed treating you so badly? With such discourtesy? Yes, I see that you did,' he concluded quietly.

Remembering the odd look she had surprised on his face at the border crossing, she asked, 'Is that why you looked, well, sort of haunted when we stopped for that meal?'

'Haunted?' he echoed softly. With a penetrating look, which she didn't in the least understand, he finally said, 'Perhaps. Certainly my behaviour was nothing to be proud of—but you do so goad me,' he added with quirky humour. 'Although, whatever else I may think of you, I cannot fault your courage.' With a gentle smile, he touched one finger to her cheek. 'Perhaps we should always meet in the dark, we seem to get on so much better. *Boa noite*, Katherine.'

'*Boa noite,*' she echoed confusedly as he walked away. With a tired little shake of her head, not entirely sure she hadn't been patronised, but much too weary to work out his odd behaviour now, she closed the door and stumbled towards the bathroom.

After a quick wash and cleaning her teeth, she returned to the bedroom and tumbled naked into the wide bed and was instantly asleep.

She was woken late the next morning by a pretty little maid bringing her a cup of coffee and drawing the deep red brocade curtains that matched those looped back either side of the bed.

'*Bom dia, senhora,*' she greeted with a rather shy smile.

'*Bom dia,*' Kate replied with a wide yawn and a smile of her own as she hoisted herself upright.

'Senhor Carlos asks if you will breakfast with him,' she explained slowly and with obvious care as though she had learned the phrase and was afraid of forgetting the words.

'Carlos?' Who the devil was Carlos? 'Who? Er—Carlos is?' she tried hopefully. Seeing that the little maid didn't understand, she shook her head. 'It doesn't matter, *não importante,*' she said triumphantly as she remembered one of Adriao's phrases. 'Thank you—er—*obrigada.*'

When she had showered she stared at the grubby jeans she had worn the previous day. There were mud stains at the knee and grass and dust stains on the rear. Well, she had nothing else to wear until Adriao retrieved her suitcases, so, with a moue of distaste, she dragged them reluctantly on. Forcing her feet into her muddy sandals, she quickly buttoned her cream shirt and followed the maid along the corridor and into a set of rooms which had clearly been turned into a self-contained apartment. A grey-haired man was sitting in front of the wide-open windows, his back to her, the table before him laid for breakfast at one end, the other covered in papers. With no idea who he was, whether he was related to Adriao, or was an employee, she approached cautiously, her face once more set into its customary mask. When nothing happened, she gave a little cough.

With a start, as though he had not heard her approach, he swung round, and a look of surprise crossed his face. He said something quickly in his own language, shook his head as if to clear it, then gave a rather embarrassed smile and got to his feet. Advancing on her, his smile turned to a grin, and, spreading his arms wide as though she were an old and valued friend instead of a complete stranger, he kissed her gently on both cheeks, then held her away to look at her, his dark eyes twinkling with amusement. 'So you are Kate! Peter and Isabella have told me of you and it is my great pleasure to meet you.'

'And mine,' she said awkwardly, not quite sure how to respond. Now that she could see his face more clearly, he didn't seem to be as old as his grey hair indicated. But he did look as though he was ill. His face was far too white and dark circles were smudged below his eyes. Suddenly aware that she was staring, she gave a small, embarrassed smile. 'How are you?' she mumbled with ridiculous formality, considering the warmth of his own greeting.

'Me?' he asked comically, indicating that she should sit. 'Me, I am in fine shape. It is you who needs the concern, I think.' With roguish amusement, he continued, 'Adriao explained what has happened and asks me to tell you that he has gone to make arrangements for your car. He tells me that you are not quite *simpático* and it was therefore a surprise for you to see him on the ferry?'

'Shock might be nearer the mark!' she exclaimed without thinking as she poured coffee for them both at his invitation.

'You were not pleased to see each other again?' he asked with such bland innocence that she couldn't help laughing, suddenly at ease with this gentle-looking man.

'You obviously know quite a bit about it,' she commented tentatively. 'But, no, we were not pleased to see each other again. In fact we spent the whole journey sniping at each other.'

'Ah, he was too busy arguing——'

'I was too busy arguing, you mean. Adriao doesn't argue, he just looks superior.'

With a shout of laughter, Carlos squeezed her hand, dispelling her chagrin at being so blunt. 'But my Adriao is superior. Do you not think so?'

'No, I don't!' she said shortly. 'And I'm sorry if it upsets you, but I find him the most arrogant, infuriating——'

'And you are not?' he teased.

'No! Well, only with him,' she qualified ruefully, then grinned enchantingly when he chuckled. And, as so often happened with older people, she relaxed and was herself. The person that so few people ever saw. Warm and charming, gentle.

'And if you smiled at my nephew like that,' Carlos commented softly, 'his arrogance would have melted like snow in the sunshine.'

'I doubt it,' she denied, yet was unable to stop the soft blush that rose to her cheeks as she remembered his strange behaviour of the night before. 'He thinks I'm ... Well, it doesn't matter what he thinks,' she mumbled hastily. 'He is your nephew?'

'But yes, he did not tell you of me?'

'Well, no. But then I wasn't expecting to come here. Nor would I be here now if it weren't for him over-ruling everything I said! You wouldn't have been so enamoured of him either if you could have seen him on the crossing, arrogance and breeding in every magnificent inch of him.' Yet he had apologised, hadn't he?

'You do admit to his magnificence, then?' he teased.

'Oh, yes, there's no denying that,' she agreed, her eyes clearly reflecting her confusion. He was magnificent—and totally infuriating.

'No,' he echoed. Then nodding towards the table, he urged, 'Help yourself to breakfast, you must be hungry.' As Kate did so, he continued quietly, 'You know that Isabella, Peter's wife, is my daughter?'

'No! Oh, hell, Peter didn't say. Why doesn't anybody ever tell me anything?' she complained.

Chuckling again, he gave her hand a comforting pat. Then, sobering, he continued gently, 'It is not my place to say, nor to interfere, but I thought perhaps I should mention that I too know all about the publicity... No, no, please let me finish. It was not my wish to censure you, just to explain that I knew, to save you any awkwardness, should the subject come up. People can be such fools, always ready to believe the worst without studying the facts.'

Staring at him in some confusion, she asked slowly, 'Are you saying that you don't believe the newspaper articles?'

'Of course I do not believe them! Why should I? Jackals, every one of them! If they do not have a story to tell, they make one up! Believe me, Kate, you have my every sympathy and support!' Suddenly re-calling himself, he gave a shamefaced smile. 'See how old men ramble on? My apologies, *senhora*, it was not my intention to open more wounds, to hurt you. You have, I think, been hurt enough.'

'Your nephew doesn't think so!' she couldn't help retorting bitterly.

'My nephew, for all his cleverness, can be a fool.' With a surprisingly conspiratorial smile, he indicated for her to continue eating.

Surprised and rather touched that a complete stranger should prove her champion, she smiled warmly at him. 'Adriao thinks Peter is a fool for believing in me.'

'Then that makes Adriao the fool,' he contradicted.

'You don't know that. You have only Peter and Isabella's word, and Adriao's differing opinion——'

'Oh, no, Adriao has not discussed it. Only Isabella, telling me Adriao's reactions. She also finds them amusing. She likes and admires you very much, Kate.'

'I like her too,' she confessed. Smiling faintly as she recalled the ebullient Isabella, she suddenly grinned. 'I'm not too sure about her wretch of a husband, though. It's beginning to seem as though he sent me out here for his own amusement.'

'Ah, no, how can you say so?' he asked with an innocent smile. 'Not that Adriao gave me any details—as you probably know, Adriao does not gossip! Unfortunately,' he tacked on with another grin.

'No, well, he wouldn't, would he?' she asked with a trace of waspishness. 'Mr Perfection wouldn't do anything so ill-bred as gossip, or only when it suits his purpose.'

Laughing delightedly, he asked, 'How ever did you manage to keep from throttling him on the drive?'

'With a great deal of difficulty!' she retorted with a grin of her own. 'Mind, to be fair, I think it was much what he wanted. He said he'd like to see me hung, drawn and quartered—only he said it as though he were merely asking me the time. So much control is not good for a man.' Although he hadn't been so controlled after the crash, had he? And then again, while they'd been walking, he'd actually been quite nice. More than nice. 'Ah, well,' she said ruefully, 'I will try not to disrupt your entire household in the short time I'm here.'

'You are not staying?' he asked, surprised.

'Would you?' she asked wryly.

'Now, Kate, how can you bear to deprive me of untold entertainment? A poor old man with nothing to do all day but gaze at his papers! You could not be so cruel.'

'Want to bet? And I certainly don't need you to stir me up—although I will endeavour not to actually come to blows with him.'

'Coming to blows might be the very thing to clear the air.'

'I doubt it. He wouldn't hit me back, you see.'

'And is that why you goad him? In an effort to provoke him into violence?'

'Good heavens, no!' she exclaimed, genuinely shocked, and then wondered in even more shock if he weren't right. 'No,' she repeated firmly, refusing even to admit to the possibility. 'He just puts my back up. But I will try to be restrained and ladylike while he's showing me round,' she promised. She doubted she'd succeed, but, still, one ought to be optimistic. 'If, that is, he hasn't already found someone to deputise for him,' she added, her lovely eyes alight with laughter.

'No, he won't do that; Adriao take his responsibilities very seriously,' he said quietly, and just for a moment a shadow moved in his dark eyes. Determinedly banishing whatever it was that had briefly troubled him, he prompted gently, 'So now tell me how you managed, with all the publicity and intrusion. If you can bear to, that is.'

'Oh, much as I always do,' she said airily. Then looking at him properly, seeing the ready sympathy in his eyes, she realised that she wanted to talk. Needed to, perhaps, and then maybe she could push it from her mind. 'It wasn't very nice,' she said. In fact, it had been decidedly mucky.

'What fools people are,' Carlos exclaimed sadly. 'Tell me about this Jean Barham I read about who left you her money and house. You knew her well?'

'Fairly well. She lived not far from me, we used to exchange pleasantries in the local shop. Just general chit-chat, you know? When I didn't see her for a while, and no one seemed to know where she was, I was worried about her. So I went round to her house. She'd had a stroke. The doctor called in most days, and the district nurse. She had a home help come in each morning, but there was no one to keep an eye on her in the afternoons or evenings, get her anything she might need. She was so terrified of being put in a home,' she said sadly.

'And her daughter?'

'Her daughter visited her once,' she said neutrally.

'So you took it upon yourself to visit her,' Carlos stated with a gentle smile.

'Mmm. She knew she wasn't going to get better,' she said sadly. 'Didn't want to get better, I don't think. She knew about the——'

'The centre?' Carlos put in helpfully.

'Yes,' she mumbled. 'How did you know? I've deliberately kept very quiet about it because the legalities aren't settled yet.'

'Isabella told me, in confidence I promise you, about how you plan to take in old people and disturbed children to give their families a break.'

'Mmm. Well, Jean knew about it, and she knew I wouldn't accept anything for myself, so she left everything to me in her will to be used to help fund the centre. If it ever gets off the ground,' she added despondently. It seemed to be taking forever. 'Lord, you wouldn't believe the rules and regulations that have to be complied with.'

'And you don't want to damage your chances with a premature announcement.'

'No,' she agreed quietly. 'It's all above board.'

'You think I doubted it?' he asked gently.

'Why shouldn't you? You don't know me...'

'I don't need to, you only have to look in your eyes to see truth and integrity there,' he argued.

'But isn't that the trade mark of the true con artist?' she protested in confusion.

'Perhaps, but Isabella is no fool, and I've known Peter a long time, I would trust his judgement over anyone. Such a collector of lame ducks is my newfound friend Kate, hmm?' he teased. 'So, despite the fact that her daughter did not visit, or care for her mother, she still expected to inherit?'

'Yes. She was furious, and when she couldn't get the will overturned she went to the newspapers, and, although they reported it, supposedly factually, they didn't know why Jean had left me the house and the money, only that she had.'

'And insinuated that you had practically blackmailed the old lady into leaving it to you.'

'Mmm. As an incident on its own, it wouldn't have been remarkable, but coming so soon after an elderly lady I'd been looking after at home on an unofficial basis left me her savings, the Press had a field day.'

'Yes, and especially as you were already a wealthy young woman in your own right. Poor Kate. And of course you didn't try to explain, justify yourself, your actions, did you?' he asked gently.

'No. Why should I? Although Peter did want to write to the papers, but my solicitor advised against it until everything was settled. Anyway, I shouldn't have to justify it. It isn't anyone's business but mine.'

'Any more than you want it justified to my nephew?'

'No,' she agreed awkwardly. 'And you obviously never discussed it with him.'

'No—when I once brought the subject up, he refused to talk about it. I didn't understand why then.'

'And now you do?' she asked, perplexed.

'Oh, yes, I think I do,' he said with a small amused smile. Patting her hand with an avuncular gesture when she continued to look confused, he added teasingly, 'Want me to play devil's advocate?'

'No! If he wants to believe me a mercenary little old lady killer, let him! That's his problem, not mine!'

'Not even a little hint?'

'No! If he didn't believe Peter, he's not likely to believe anyone else, is he? And if you do mention it, he'll only think I've been pleading my cause.'

'All right, Kate,' he agreed, giving her hand another little pat. 'I won't tell him.'

'Tell me what?' Adriao asked softly from behind them.

Swinging round with a little start, she glared at him, and he gave a small unamused smile. He was dressed in an exquisitely cut dark grey suit over a light grey shirt, a dark red tie making the only splash of colour. He looked formal, and remote, aloof, and he held her eyes for long moments, confusing her, until, with a little dip of his head, he greeted smoothly, '*Bom dia,* Katherine, Carlos.' Touching his uncle's shoulder affectionately in passing, he added, 'Is the coffee fresh?'

'Yes,' she said stiffly, her eyes lowered. 'Would you like a cup?'

'Please.' Taking the seat opposite, he watched her, his face still.

'Do you want a roll?'

'But no, I have already breakfasted,' he said smoothly, making it sound as though he thought she should have done so also and she glanced up, her lips tight, her easy relaxed mood with Carlos disappearing as though it had never been.

Taking refuge in aggression, as she normally did, because here in his own home he seemed more a stranger, more remote, she asked bluntly, 'You have sorted out about the car?'

'I have. It has been towed to a garage, and your luggage and belongings are in your room.'

'Thank you.'

'Ah, so you are staying with us after all,' Carlos exclaimed with satisfaction.

'No, I'm not,' she said defiantly, her eyes still held by Adriao's. 'I have a room booked at the Palace Hotel in Porto—— '

'No, you haven't,' Adriao denied quietly. 'The room wasn't guaranteed and when you didn't arrive last night they let it to someone else.'

'Damn. Oh, well, I don't suppose it matters, there are other hotels—— ' Breaking off, she stared at

Adriao in exasperation as he slowly shook his head. 'What's that supposed to mean?'

'It means, dear Kate, that there are no other hotels, at least none near enough, and even those will be fully booked at this time of year. Besides, I have no intention of contravening the race rules. No, Kate, you will have to stay here.'

'But I don't want to stay here! Surely the rules will allow me to stay near by?'

With another little shake of his head, mockery in every damned line of him, he finally looked away and began to pour himself more coffee.

Turning to glance at his uncle, she said helplessly, 'Carlos?'

'It is true, Kate, the rules do state that you have to stay here. Do you hate the thought so much of being here with me?'

'No, of course not! Not with you! Him! We'll probably turn the house into a battlefield!'

'What an enchanting prospect,' Adriao commented with a droll look and Kate gave another grunt of exasperation.

'Why don't you show Kate round?' Carlos asked his nephew blandly, and Kate could have hit him. He was doing it on purpose, the wretch. But, if he thought he could throw them together for his own amusement, he had another think coming.

'I'm sure Adriao has more than enough to occupy him without having to bother with me,' she pointed out tartly.

'Now, why should you think that, Katherine?' he asked, that horrid amusement lurking in his eyes. 'It will be my pleasure to show you round my home.'

She didn't miss the none too subtle emphasis on it being his home either, even if Carlos did. 'Thank you,' she said sweetly, 'you're too kind.'

'Yes,' he agreed softly and for two pins she could have kicked him under the table.

'You said you had a meeting this morning.'

'I do. Later.'

Her mouth pursed, she glanced at Carlos and saw a small smile playing about his mouth, a look of quiet satisfaction in his eyes. 'You're enjoying this, aren't you?' she demanded, suddenly uncaring what anyone thought.

'Yes, my dear Kate, I have to confess I am.'

With a very unladylike snort, she finished her coffee and got to her feet. 'If you gentlemen will excuse me, I would like to go and change out of these crumpled clothes.'

'But of course, Katherine,' Adriao replied smoothly. 'I will wait for you in the hall.'

Feeling unaccountably depressed, she went up to her room and changed into a soft pale blue shift dress that would be cool and comfortable.

'What is Carlos not to tell me?' Adriao asked quietly some half-hour later as he led the way up a winding stone staircase into one of the turrets.

'Nothing!' she denied shortly. 'How much further is it?'

'Not far,' he said mildly, before continuing as though he hadn't been interrupted, 'Because I feel I should in all honesty warn you that Carlos has nothing of his own to leave. Nothing of any great value, that is. I shouldn't want you to waste your time.'

'I never waste my time—and I don't want Carlos to leave me anything,' she denied. So that was the interpretation he'd put on her words, was it? Typical. Did he think her mind revolved solely on what possessions people had and what chance she'd have of getting her sticky fingers on them? Obviously he did, although how the devil he thought she'd had time to con his uncle in the short time they'd been together she didn't know. Staring at the broad back and strong legs disappearing ahead of her, she stuck her tongue out at him. 'I liked him,' she said defiantly, as though that had some bearing on the case.

'So I gathered. Do I take it from your tone that you find it extraordinary that any relative of mine could actually be nice?'

'If the cap fits! Has he been ill?' she asked more quietly. 'I didn't think he looked at all well.'

'Hoping he might change his will before he turns up his toes?' he asked in that same infuriatingly polite voice. There was something so unsettling, she thought crossly, about being insulted politely!

'No, I do not! My God, Adriao, you have a rotten mind! I was merely observing that I thought he looked ill!'

'Were you?' he asked, and suddenly he sounded indescribably weary, and she stared at him in further confusion. Would she ever understand him? she wondered. Did she even want to?

Halting, he looked down at her. 'He has been ill,' he admitted. 'That's why I insisted he came to live with me.'

'Insisted?' she queried, and suddenly remembered the shadow she'd seen in his uncle's eyes. 'He didn't want to come?'

'He didn't want to impose . . .'

'Oh.'

'And doesn't,' he added, presumably in case she might think otherwise.

'No,' she agreed softly. Still searching Adriao's face, she asked quietly, 'How ill has he been?' If he was really ill, it would be the height of stupidity for her to stay. He might find her and Adriao's wrangling amusing, but it could also be very wearying for someone not in full health.

With a little sigh, he lowered himself to sit on one of the steps, bringing his face almost level with hers, and she hastily leaned back. An action not unnoticed by Adriao, who gave a nasty little smile. 'His heart is not strong,' he informed her without expression, 'and a few months ago he had a slight stroke, but so long as he rests, takes things quietly, has no worries, there is no reason why he should not live to a ripe old age.'

'I see,' she commented as she tried to flatten herself further against the wall without his noticing. She seemed to be having trouble with her breathing too and tried to convince herself it was because of the steep climb. Only of course it wasn't. It was the fact of his leaning so closely towards her.

His eyes narrowing on her face, he approved quietly, 'Good, because if you hurt him, or upset him in any way, you will be very, very sorry.'

'I have no intention of upsetting him!' she retorted angrily. 'Stop being so damned suspicious! Does he know about his heart?'

'Yes.'

'He didn't say,' she murmured. 'Well, that settles it,' she declared strongly, 'it would be much better all round if I found a hotel.'

'Would it? Why?' he asked with that haughty lift of his eyebrow that she found so infuriating.

'Because obviously my staying here——'

'My dear Kate, what possible difference can it make to him? Apart from enjoying your company, that is. He doesn't have to cook your meals, make your bed——'

'I didn't say he did! I just meant having a guest in the house... Especially me,' she added morosely. 'If he needs peace and quiet...'

'Oh, a bit of gentle stimulation won't hurt him,' he said blandly.

'I am not known,' she pointed out acidly, 'for providing gentle stimulation. 'Anyway, I would have thought you'd be the last person to want me to stay.'

'Why? Because we dislike each other? Besides, I already told you, I need you to stay until Peter arrives——'

'Oh, yes, the race rules,' she finished for him with a little grimace.

'As you say. Come,' he added, getting to his feet, 'I will finish showing you round. Carlos might ask questions,' he warned blandly.

'What happened to his wife?' she asked curiously as she began following him again. 'Or does she live here too? I don't recall Isabella ever mentioning her mother.'

'No,' he denied unhelpfully.

'No what?' she asked irritably. 'No, he doesn't have a wife? Or, no, she doesn't live here?'

'Both,' he said flatly. 'She died some years ago.'

Making it quite clear that the subject was now closed, he continued on up the steps. Following him resentfully, she came out on to what she could only suppose were called the battlements. Leaning her elbows on the crumbling ledge, she stared out over the Douro valley. The wind was stronger up here, tugging her short hair violently awry, ruffling Adriao's across his forehead. Far below she could see the winding river, a long blue snake, sparkling in the sunshine. Pine forests, small red-roofed dwellings dotted around like children's toys. 'It's beautiful,' she approved grudgingly, her words snatched away on the wind, and wished perversely that she could find something disparaging to say about it.

She didn't know if Adriao heard, or maybe understood what she was thinking from her expression, because he gave a small, sour smile. Leaning with his back against the chest-high embrasure, he watched her, not the view.

'I know Carlos thinks it will amuse him to hear us squabble like fractious children,' he began, his voice pitched loud enough for her to hear easily. 'But——'

'You don't squabble, I do,' she pointed out without looking at him. 'And I doubt the elegant Adriao Carvalho Ferreira does anything so commonplace as sound fractious.'

'Do you, Katherine? But then you know so very little about me.'

'I know a lot of things about you,' she quipped lightly.

'And to all my detriment, no doubt...'

'No. Not all,' she murmured as she remembered his gentleness of the night before, his enthusiasm for his country.

Finding that she didn't want to discuss the finer points of his personality, she returned her gaze to the view. Idly watching a bird wheel about the blue, blue sky, she allowed the warmth of the sun to soothe her, and, whether it was the warm air, the view, or the atmosphere of the old castle, or maybe even learning of Carlos's frailty, all of a sudden she no longer felt irritated or self-conscious. No longer felt like snapping at Adriao's heels like a bewildered terrier, and at the odd analogy her mouth tugged into a wry grin.

'Are you happy, Katherine?' he asked abruptly, startling her.

'Happy?' she asked slowly as she turned towards him. 'Yes, I suppose so. I've never really thought about it. Apart from the current contretemps with the Barhams, I'm quite content. Why did you ask? I can't really believe you're even remotely interested in my feelings.'

'Only perhaps in so far as they may affect Carlos. I would prefer us to at least attempt a harmonious relationship while you are here. Will you try? For my uncle's sake?'

Turning, and leaning as he was, her back to the view, she nodded. 'Yes, of course. I have no wish to upset him either. I don't always mean to be rude, you know. I start out with such good intentions, not to be ruffled by you, not to over-react, only...'

'You do not need to tell me the "only", Katherine,' he commented drily. 'I know the "only", too well. Come, it is too windy up here for intelligent conversation; we'll go down to the terrace and I will show you the vineyards.' With a smile that was very difficult for her to read, he led the way down.

'How old is the castle?' she asked curiously, as she carefully negotiated the crumbling steps.

'This part dates back to the fifteenth century, the main house is later, maybe seventeenth, and it isn't really a castle, originally it was a Benedictine monastery, very spartan and uncomfortable,' he derided over his shoulder.

'But not now. Or at least, not the living quarters...'

'No, my ancestors, like myself, abhorred being spartan or uncomfortable,' he mocked. 'Your room is to your liking?'

'Yes, thank you, the bed is very comfortable.'

'I'm pleased to hear it.'

'Even if the—er—appointments, are rather formal for my taste,' she concluded with a little smile as she recalled the heavy wooden furniture and sombre prints on the white walls.

'Ah, praise tempered by disparagement, just to keep me in my place,' he murmured and Kate laughed.

'I very much doubt you need keeping in your place. You always give the impression of knowing your place to the very last inch.'

'And expecting others to know it too?' he taunted, halting to look up at her.

'Yes,' she agreed defiantly, her eyes determinedly holding his. 'And why, might I ask, are you being so tolerant of me all of a sudden? Carlos isn't around to hear us.'

'Because, Miss Lassiter, I have beautiful manners and it would be discourteous to be rude to a guest in my home.' With that funny little lift of his eyebrows, as though questioning her reaction, he turned and continued down.

Pulling a face at his arrogant back, she moved after him. 'And you really don't need to keep emphasising the fact that it is your home and not your uncle's,' she reproved. 'I do get the point, you know.'

'I'm very glad to hear it; so tedious having to repeat oneself all the time.'

Startled into a snort of unexpected laughter, she slipped past him, and walked quietly along the hall and through the heavy door at the end. The wide terrace ran the width of the house, the trellised arches laden with some sort of vine, purple trumpet flowers clustered thickly on their stems, the light perfume redolent of wallflowers. 'Mmm, nice,' she exclaimed softly, more to herself than to her companion. 'A hell of an improvement on London.'

'Yes. You will excuse me for a moment? I will arrange for cool drinks to be brought.'

When he'd gone, slipping quietly away, she walked to where Carlos was sitting, papers spread out on a long table before him, a frown on his face.

'You're looking very solemn,' she teased. 'What are you doing? Cooking the books?'

'If by that very odd phrase you mean am I doing something I shouldn't, then no,' he said leaning back to smile at her. 'I am trying to finalise details for this damned race!'

'Oh, so it's a damned race now, is it? When I rubbished it, I got put very firmly in my place,' she retorted, a good deal amused. Resting her back against one of the pergola uprights, she ordered softly, 'Tell me about it.'

Looking at her sideways from the corner of his eye, he suddenly grinned and leaned back. 'The Port Lodge Race,' he began pompously, 'is to be held in just over two weeks' time. Teams from the seven major wine lodges are to race from Porto to wherever by whichever route they choose.'

'To wherever?' she asked with a quizzical smile. 'Don't you know where they're going?'

'No, no one will know until one minute before the start. No maps, no directions, just the ultimate destination.'

'Sounds fun. And good old Peter and Adriao are taking part?'

'Yes.'

Her tongue very firmly in her cheek, she exclaimed softly, 'Well, I hope they take a mechanic along with them.'

Laughing delightedly, he swept some papers off the other chair and indicated for her to sit. 'I think perhaps Adriao is not quite so ignorant of mechanics as he would have you believe. Are you?' he asked his nephew as he returned to the terrace carrying a tray of drinks.

As Adriao's eyes met hers, she knew he was remembering her caustic comments when he'd been peering into the engine of her car, and then he gave a slow, extremely devastating smile, his eyes crinkling attractively at the corners, and she forgot for a moment what the conversation had been about. Staring at him, rather bemused, she blinked and looked away when he answered.

'Not entirely,' he denied softly. Unable to put the tray on the table for the papers, he put it on the flagstones then handed Kate a long frosted glass of amber-coloured liquid before passing one to his uncle.

'Fruit drink. *Sumo de frutas*,' he informed her. 'Very thirst quenching. So, when you are out, you will say, *um sumo de frutas, se faz favor*.'

'Will I?' she asked, still rather shaken by his smile, and, not for the first time, began to wonder if she hadn't seriously misjudged this rather unsettling man. Certainly she'd seriously misjudged the effect he could have on her.

'But of course. Oh, and before I forget, I have arranged a hire car for you.' Delving into his pocket, he withdrew some keys and dropped them into her lap. 'You have insurance to cover it?'

'Yes, I took out five-star cover; do you need the credit vouchers now?'

'No, when it is returned to the garage will do, and when I return from my meeting I will come with you to try it out. So——'

'Adriao,' she interrupted with a trace of asperity. 'I've been driving for some years. I'm quite capable of trying it out by myself.'

With a look that might be used to quell infants, and quite ignoring her protest, he continued blandly, 'So now we will discuss where you are to visit for your article.'

'Oh, I am allowed to go touring round, then? I kind of got the impression I'd been incarcerated in the castle for the duration.'

'No, Kate,' he said softly, a rather odd expression in his eyes, as though he was laughing at her, 'I only need for this to be your place of residence until Peter arrives. So, do you have any particular places in mind?'

'No,' she denied as she tried to match his offhand tone, 'I thought I would leave it to you.'

'Of course,' he agreed with an arrogance that shouldn't have astonished her, but did. 'That is understood.'

'You're joking.'

'Joking? Why should I be joking?'

'Because, Adriao, I am quite capable of deciding where I want to go, and going there.'

'Not alone, you aren't.'

'Of course I am! I've been junketing about Europe on my own for years!'

'But now you are no longer alone. Are you?' he asked. His tone might have been soft, conversational, but there was most definitely a warning in those dark

eyes that returned her gaze so steadily. 'You will need
to visit the major towns, Braga, Viano do Castello,
Porto, the wine caves, naturally...'

'Naturally,' she murmured with a sarcasm that was
entirely wasted. 'And the vineyards...'

'Oh, well, those you can see from here,' he said
casually, waving one arm over the veranda rail. 'It is
not so much to see, one vineyard is much like another
to...'

'An ignoramus,' she put in helpfully when he
paused to search for an appropriate word.

'Determined I should insult your intelligence, Kate?'

'No,' she denied flatly, 'being determined is
obviously going to be a complete and utter waste of
time. On my part, that is,' she added sweetly. 'Go
on.'

A gleam of mockery in his eyes, he continued
blandly, 'I was merely going to say that the wine lodges
in Porto would be interesting, to see where the grapes
end up, where the port is made for export, and port
wine for our home consumption.'

'I see. Sounds riveting,' she said in a dry little voice.

'Oh, it is, Kate. It is,' he returned softly.

In order to disguise the little twitch of her lips, she
bent her head and began to sip her fruit juice.

'I have unfortunately to be in a meeting for the rest
of the day—you can amuse yourself?'

'Oh, I'm sure I can find something to do,' she murmured with a bit of gentle mockery of her own. 'I'm
a big girl now, I don't need you to wait on me. But
it was kind of you to be concerned.'

'No, it wasn't,' he denied solemnly, his amusement
betrayed only by the slightest quiver in his voice. 'As
you have no doubt already noticed, I have beautiful
manners.'

This time she was quite unable to suppress her twitching mouth. Her eyes gleaming, she murmured softly, 'Well, that successfully put me in my place. Are you going to your wine cave?'

'No, and it is not my wine cave. It is a co-operative shared between three of us major vineyard holders.' Holding her eyes, he asked softly, 'Are you flirting with me, Kate?'

As she stared at him, her amusement fled and she blushed scarlet. 'No!' she exclaimed.

'Ah. I'm very pleased to hear it, because it did occur to me that perhaps I had been going about things in the wrong way.' His eyes capturing and holding hers, a fascinating smile dancing in their depths, he continued softly, 'Had I asked, instead of demanding, would you have agreed to stay willingly, I wonder?'

'No,' she denied, which was untrue. If he had smiled, and asked her like that, she'd have moved in like a shot—and hated herself for the admission, because that smacked of lack of will-power, of behaving like some sort of bimbo, willing to give up all for a man's approval. With a little snort, she repeated more firmly, 'No.'

With a small smile, he turned away, and, leaning his shoulders against one of the uprights, looked out over the garden. 'I will explain,' he continued, his voice even, disinterested almost, and any feelings of burgeoning warmth she might have felt were instantly dispelled. She would be very, very careful in future not to give him the chance to level any more like accusations at her, she determined, her mouth tight. Flirting indeed! He was probably so spoilt by constant adulation that he found it inconceivable that any woman could actually dislike him.

Peeping sideways at Carlos, she hastily looked away when she saw he was watching her, unholy amusement dancing in his eyes. Dragging her attention to Adriao's soft voice, she made a determined effort to pay attention. 'And you will see when you are out that most dwellings have some vines, even if only one or two. All the grapes are collected together; all, no matter how poor, are part of the whole wine programme. Myself and two other families are directors of the lodge, but the profits are shared by all. You understand?'

'Yes,' she said hastily and very firmly in case anyone should doubt it.

'Well, it is very complicated, but, if you are really interested, I will explain it to you when we have more time. But now I really must go to my meeting.' Turning to face her, he gave a slight smile. 'Of the building committee, of which I am a member. We try to ensure that all new building work conforms to our standards. We do not always succeed,' he finished drily.

The look on his face indicated exactly the opposite, and she gave him a small, disbelieving smile. She doubted he'd lose anything he'd set his mind to winning! In fact it was probably a case of woe betide anyone who got in his way! Something she might do well to remember herself!

'What a busy little bee you are,' she derided tartly. 'Vine grower, director of a lodge, director of tourism, and now a building committee.'

'You forgot reluctant guide,' he told her as he straightened. With his autocratic little dip of the head, he turned and left.

Exasperated, she waited until he was out of earshot before demanding of his uncle, 'Does he treat all women as though they're four years old and backward? I do so hate to be patronised!'

'He wasn't patronising you, Kate,' Carlos denied. 'But oh, I am so glad you have come to stay.'

'I can see you are! It's given you a whole new lease of life! Complicated,' she spluttered. 'I bet it's not complicated at all! Why do men like that always assume that women have no understanding?'

'Kate, Kate,' Carlos soothed, 'he doesn't. Truly.'

'Yes, he does.' Pulling a face, she stared out over the valley. 'He always makes me so, so...'

'Confused?' Carlos asked gently.

'Yes,' she admitted.

'Well, don't let it worry you,' he comforted. 'From what I can gather, he seems to confuse most women, but I don't honestly think he was trying to be provocative just now; he was, I think, what do you say in your country? Pulling your foot?'

'Leg,' she corrected automatically with a rather bewildered frown. No, she was sure he hadn't been teasing her. Or had he? It wasn't in the least easy to tell with Adriao—he never gave any indication of what he might be thinking.

'Don't worry about it, my Kate,' Carlos soothed. 'Perhaps it was merely that his mind was on his forthcoming meeting. It is important to him, the preservation of our valleys. He is a little over-zealous perhaps, but that is not a bad fault. I could wish that others felt the same, but I am sure he was not really putting you down, just not perhaps thinking what he was saying.'

Which was hardly flattering, she thought with a wry smile. Turning to Carlos, she grinned. 'Sorry, I shouldn't talk about your nephew like that, should I?'

'Why? We are all entitled to our own opinions, Kate. Now, you will give me the pleasure of your company over lunch?'

When they had eaten, and while Carlos returned to his rooms for his afternoon sleep, she decided to explore her immediate surroundings, and never mind Adriao's instruction that she stay put. She wasn't a child, for heaven's sake, and quite capable of driving round for a few hours without mishap. Anyway, she wanted to try out the hire car. An estate, similar to her own, she discovered, and she smiled. If she had expected anything, it would have been that he had got her a small Fiat or something. Perhaps, as Carlos said, she did misjudge him. Or misunderstand him; he was after all speaking to her in what was for him a foreign language. Perhaps he didn't always use the right words. Yeah, and perhaps pigs really did fly.

Scribbling a note for Carlos, and leaving it in a prominent place, she collected her bag and went out to the car. Consulting the map, she decided to head for Penafiel, and, depending how long that took her, perhaps recross the river at Marco Canaveses and back down to the *castelo*. Running a brush through her hair, and making sure she had some money, she set off. As Adriao had said, the area was beautiful. The sun was shining, she seemed to have come to a better understanding with Adriao, or at least a shaky truce, people in the little villages she passed through all waved and smiled at her, and, all in all, she decided she hadn't made a mistake in coming after all.

She noticed the vines in almost every plot of land and she smiled; it must be nice to think you were a part of the great overall export plan, however many grapes you contributed. There was a great deal of poverty, yet no one looked miserable or downtrodden. Being poor in a warm climate was a hell of a lot better than being poor in somewhere wet and cold.

The roads wound lazily up and down and the only traffic she encountered were ancient old farm trucks that looked as though they were about to fall to pieces, a herd of goats being driven wherever, and the local bus. One hell of a route he had, she thought as she was waved past. It only took an hour to reach Penafiel and she parked in the small town square and went to have a cool drink, ordering, as instructed by Adriao, *um sumo de frutas*. She'd forgotten that the shops closed in the afternoons, so, instead of wandering round as she had intended, she lingered over her drink and watched the world go by.

Timing herself nicely, she arrived back at the village below the *castelo* as the church clock was striking six. Plenty of time to shower and change before dinner, and all would have been well if, just as she reached the bend, a rusty old blue truck hadn't shot out backwards in front of her. Slamming on her brakes, she watched in horror as it continued across the verge and through the pine trees. All that stood between it and a two-hundred-foot drop to the river below were spindly pines. Swerving on to the verge, she braked and climbed hastily out. Two men were running across the road in the direction from which the truck had come, and others, she saw, were beginning to appear. Ignoring them for the moment, she walked cautiously towards the truck. It had come to a precarious rest, its rear hanging over the drop, the cab precisely placed between two of the trees.

What damnable luck, she thought. An inch to either side and the trees would have stopped it. Two frightened faces peered through the windscreen. Children. They couldn't get out because of the close proximity of the trees either side preventing the door from opening, or anyone getting them through the window. And presumably trying to smash the windscreen might send the truck hurtling over the edge. Feeling sick, she ran back to her car to collect the towing chain she'd seen there when she'd first checked the car out. She was accompanied by the two men she'd seen first. Handing one end to them, she attached the other end to the towing bar. Pausing only long enough to check that they'd attached their end, she climbed behind the wheel and started the engine. Engaging drive, and sending up a swift prayer, she turned the wheel hard to take her diagonally across the road in a straight line on the truck. Noticing thankfully that a few people had spread across the road to either side of her to warn off any other traffic, she edged slowly forward until she felt the chain grow taut. With one man walking beside her open window giving hand directions, she kept a steady pressure on the accelerator. Without warning, the car shot forward and she hastily rammed her foot on the brake.

Surely the damned chain hadn't broken? Turning in her seat, she peered backwards unable to make out from the wild gesticulating and shouting what the hell had happened. Sticking her head out of the window, she yelled, 'What?' Oh, damn it, what was Portuguese for 'what'? *Que?* Oh, what the hell. *'Que?'* she shouted and got a shouted reply, which, naturally, she didn't understand. Climbing out, she went to look for herself.

Whoever had attached the chain had stupidly attached it to the bumper, which, naturally, being rusted through, had promptly come away as soon as any pressure was applied. Honestly, you always assumed men knew what the hell they were doing.

With a great many arm movements and slow speaking which didn't make their meaning any clearer, she finally grasped that they wanted to thread the chain through the axle, which it wasn't long enough to do unless she reversed. Nodding, she ran back to her car and returned to her previous position. When a fist was thumped on the roof, she began to edge forward again.

From being an empty, sleepy little village, the road was now packed. There seemed to be hundreds of people milling around and several cars and trucks parked any old how across the road. With fingers crossed, she repeated her earlier manoeuvre. Unfortunately, because the road ran downhill, as soon as the truck was clear of the trees it picked up speed, and there was nothing Kate could do but wait fatalistically for it to crash into the back of her car. The children in the cab were obviously too terrified, or not knowledgeable enough, to apply the brake. If she pulled away and round the curve in the road, the truck would crash into the house that stood foursquare on the corner. The only thing she could possibly do was hope to cushion the impact. Holding her foot on the brake, she watched through the rear-view mirror and tried to judge the moment when the truck would hit.

Surveying the rather large dent in the rear, she shrugged; a small price to pay for two children's lives, and she could easily afford to have it mended. The hire company would just have to lump it. With much hand shaking and back slapping all round, Kate finally drove up to the *castelo*.

Adriao was waiting on the doorstep, a thunderous frown on his face. Climbing out, she gave him a puzzled glance, then flinched when he said coldly,

'Is it too much to hope that you might show some consideration? You know of my uncle's heart, I told you this morning, and that he must not be worried.'

'But I haven't worried him,' she said, perplexed, 'I left him a note——'

'Yes!' he bit out. 'At two o'clock.'

'Well, I'm very sorry,' she said lamely. 'I didn't——'

Without waiting for her to finish he turned on his heel and stalked inside.

Following more slowly, her face puzzled, she walked upstairs and tapped on Carlos's door. 'I'm sorry if you were worried,' she said gently as she slipped inside after he'd answered her knock.

'I wasn't worried!' he exclaimed in surprise. 'Well, maybe a little concerned,' he qualified almost as though he thought it might be rude not to be just a little disturbed by the late return of a guest. 'It was Adriao who was worried. Do not look so upset,' he comforted with a smile. 'It truly does not matter. I expect you forgot the time.'

'Well, no, I intended to be back at six, as I said in my note, and it can't be far off that, can it?' Glancing at his wall clock, she was horrified to find it was almost seven-thirty. It surely hadn't taken an hour and a half to pull the truck free. No wonder Adriao had been so furious—and not because he'd been worried either! That she wouldn't believe. 'Oh, hell, Carlos, I'm sorry.'

'It is all right, of course it is all right. Do not look so distressed. You are on holiday, you must not consider an old man's fears.'

'Well, of course I must consider them! And I truly did not intend to be this late—and you aren't old. Only mature,' she teased as she impulsively dropped a light kiss on his hair.

'Sixty-five is old,' he corrected with a smile. 'Go and get changed, you look as though you've been rolling in the pine forest, which I trust you have not.'

'No, not quite.' With another smile, she went out and along to her room, still considerably puzzled by Adriao's behaviour. He didn't normally shout and wave his arms about in temper.

After a quick shower, Kate dressed in a flowing skirt and top in Indian cotton. Not bothering with much make-up, just a flick of mascara and lipstick, she thrust her feet into high-heeled sandals and hurried down to the dining-room.

Taking her place, she gave Carlos a quick smile, then peeped towards his nephew. The tailored black shirt he was wearing would have made him look austere and unapproachable even if he hadn't still been angry. Which he clearly was, his face set and withdrawn. So much for better relations, she thought unhappily. She glanced at him several times while they ate, yet could discover no softening in him. A frown still marred his brow as he played with the food on his plate and she felt saddened that hostilities might have resumed. She no longer wanted to fight with him, had thought, hoped, perhaps, that they might get to know each other better. With a long sigh she pushed her own unfinished plate away from her and picked up her wine glass.

Carlos apparently had more papers to go through concerning the race, and, with a quick excuse, went up to his rooms, taking his coffee with him. Without his soothing presence, the atmosphere worsened dramatically. Feeling tense and nervous, she glanced at him again. He looked so very forbidding in the muted light from the wall lamps. Dark and unapproachable. Foreign. It didn't help that the heavily framed oil-painting behind him depicted someone who looked suspiciously like a member of the Spanish Inquisition. As though feeling her scrutiny, he looked up, his eyes flat, cold, expressionless.

Unable to stand the fraught silence any longer, she flung down her napkin and said in a little burst of temper, 'I don't know why you're so angry! I've said I was sorry!'

Leaning back in his chair, he picked up his wine glass and regarded her coldly over the rim. 'I asked you not to go out on your own——'

'You didn't ask me! You told me!'

'I asked you,' he repeated. 'Is it too much to expect a little common courtesy?'

'Of course it isn't! But anyone would think I was late back on purpose, and I wasn't. It was quite unintentional!'

'As unintentional presumably as the large dent in the rear of the car?'

'Yes!' she gritted. 'And quite unavoidable!'

'And is everything you do unavoidable, Katherine?'

'Oh, for goodness' sake! Don't you think you're over-reacting?' Shoving her chair back, she stormed out to the terrace. Honestly, anyone would think she'd stolen one of his precious possessions the way he was carrying on! Gripping the old wood of the railing, she stared mutinously out over the dark garden. She didn't actually hear him come out, but knew the exact moment he came to stand behind her. Increasingly nervous for no very good reason, or no logical reason, she moved further along the terrace into the concealing darkness.

'Look, I've said I'm sorry, and I am.'

'I don't want your apology!'

'Then what do you want?' she swung round to demand, and found him a great deal closer than she either expected or wanted. Taking another nervous step backwards, she repeated, a trifle haughtily, 'Well? For me to grovel?' As he took a step towards her, she held her hand out placatingly, or warningly, she wasn't very sure which. 'I don't even know why you're so angry with me!' she burst out. 'Your uncle is all right——'

'I am angry, as you so succinctly put it,' he explained with dangerous softness, 'because I do not like to be made a fool——'

'I didn't——'

'Be quiet. After the accident yesterday, during our walk, and again this morning, I had thought I'd misjudged you, and I was sorry for it. I had thought you more maligned than malicious. Only you are not! You deliberately went out exploring! You deliberately worried my uncle, whom I told you must not be worried——' Breaking off, he swivelled swiftly round as he heard a footstep behind him. 'Sim?' he barked at the manservant who was hovering. After a short discussion, he muttered something under his breath, and, with an irritable look at Kate, accompanied the manservant back through the lounge doors.

Left alone, her temper subsided and she gazed moodily out over the valley. So much for explaining.

When he returned a few minutes later, he was carrying the towing chain from the hire car, which he dropped with a little clatter at her feet.

'One of the men from the village just returned it. He asked me to thank you again. Is it so impossible to tell me things?' he burst out. 'You only had to explain why you were late, but no, it is much better that I think badly of you, isn't it?'

'Oh, don't be so ridiculous! When I returned from the village you didn't give me a chance to explain! Just stormed off. And just now, when I was trying to tell you why I was late, you lammed into me about consideration! Is it my fault if you always assume the worst?'

Brushing past him, she went to storm inside, only to be brought to a halt by his hand on her arm.

Swinging her round, he inadvertently pulled her off balance and she fell against him, her face very close to his. Too close. Her breath jerking to a halt, she stared at him, at the bright glitter of his eyes that stared so emptily back. Felt the soft puff of his breath on her cheek as he exhaled sharply, could feel the individual pressure of each finger as he gripped her arms—and then suddenly she was free, jerked away from him and released. With a deep, gasping breath, she hurried past him and down the steps to the garden, anywhere to get away from him, from his nearness.

'Kate!'

'Go away,' she said distractedly. Hearing him behind her, she tried to hurry, and quite forgetting that the garden shelved steeply down, she lost her footing and would have fallen head first if Adriao had not grabbed her from behind. As it was, she knocked him off balance and they both went sprawling into an undignified little heap and made an unlooked-for descent through the shrubbery.

Oh, dear God, not again! Untangling herself from him, she scrabbled her way agitatedly back up, her breathing coming in angry jerks as he followed her, muttering and swearing to himself.

'Here,' he said harshly, grabbing her and pushing her on to firmer ground.

'I can manage!' she gritted.

'Then damned well manage!' he retorted furiously as he bundled her against a nearby tree. As he moved to put himself on to firmer ground, his foot slipped and he lurched against her, his hand accidentally touching her breast, his face grazing hers. With a swift indrawn hiss of breath, she reacted without thinking and shoved him away.

With a yell of alarm, he grabbed frantically at the tree and his whole weight slammed painfully into her. 'What the hell do you think you're doing? I know we've had our differences, but there's no need to try to kill me!'

'I wasn't trying to kill you!' she denied forcefully. 'I don't like being touched—and will you please get off me?'

'With pleasure!' he gritted. With a powerful thrust of his arms, he forced himself away. 'You think I would touch you by choice? Next time you can damned well save yourself!'

# CHAPTER FOUR

'THERE won't be a next time,' Kate muttered inaudibly. Kicking irritably at the tree, then slamming her hand against the rough bark in impotent temper, she glared down at the offending shrubs. Damn, damn, damn, damn! Why, she asked herself despairingly, why did she always have to over-react? Putting a shaky hand up to her face where Adriao had touched her, she drew in a quivering breath. She could still almost feel the warmth of his skin against hers, the heat of his fingers momentarily touching her breast.

And why the hell had he been so angry? It was a natural enough reaction, wasn't it? To automatically shove him away? 'You think I would touch you by choice?' he had asked scathingly. No, she didn't suppose he would, she thought miserably. And she truly didn't think she had wanted him to—until now. Didn't you, Kate? she asked herself. Wasn't it because you did want him that you shoved him away? Because you knew he didn't want you? Isn't that what this whole squabble is about?

It wasn't fair, she thought despairingly, that a man she didn't even like should make her feel like this. That her body should betray her. Sexual attraction, Kate, that's what it is. What it's always been. A war between mind and body.

Far more shaken than she should have been for such a stupid little incident, she tried to drum up a feeling of anger at his ill usage of her, and couldn't—because the whole thing had been her fault. Had always been her fault because she'd been behaving like a little girl wanting attention. Is that what he thought when he looked at her? Dear God, please don't let him think that. It would be preferable for him to think her mercenary.

Confused, aching and uncertain, she turned her head to stare up at the light spilling out on to the dark terrace from the french doors. There was no sign of Adriao—presumably he'd gone inside, and she wished with all her heart that she didn't have to follow him. With a long, unhappy sigh, she pushed herself away from the tree and carefully negotiated the dark garden. She didn't want to have to see him, have him look at her with contempt. But then neither could she hide in the garden until he'd gone to bed.

Taking a deep breath to give herself courage, she brushed herself down as best she could without being able to see what sort of mess she was in, then crossed the terrace and entered the lounge. Adriao was standing with his back to her at the bar in the corner and there was a long streak of dirt down one trouser leg, she saw. Carlos was lying at ease in one of the comfortable leather armchairs, and a young girl, a very beautiful, delicate-looking young girl was perched nervously on the edge of an upright chair against the wall. Halting awkwardly in the doorway, Kate looked from one to the other.

'I'm sorry, I didn't realise you had a guest . . .' she began hesitantly.

'Kate.' Carlos began turning to smile at her, then halted in surprise as he took in her appearance. 'Good gracious, what on earth have you two been up to?'

Giving him a shaky smile, and carefully avoiding looking anywhere near Adriao, she explained awkwardly, 'We slid over the edge of the garden, and I think we—er—ruined the shrubbery.'

Looking as though he was trying very hard not to laugh, he shook his head at her. 'You are not hurt?'

'No. I'd best go and clean myself up.'

'Yes, but first let me introduce Eleanor. Eleanor,' he said gently, 'meet Kate.'

She smiled at the young girl, who smiled nervously back, then they both jumped when Adriao unexpectedly slammed a glass down on the bar and turned.

'I'll take you home,' he said abruptly, followed by something said swiftly in his own tongue, and Eleanor got meekly to her feet, her eyes downcast. She looked as though she was about to burst into tears.

When they'd gone, Carlos gave Kate's unhappy face a searching glance, then suddenly smiled. 'What did you do to my nephew?'

'I didn't do anything,' she denied quietly as she absently brushed at the pieces of tree bark adhering to the front of her skirt.

'You didn't?' he asked in disbelief.

'No. Well,' she qualified with a sheepish smile as she glanced at him beneath her lashes, 'I sort of slipped off the edge of the garden, and when he tried to save me, we both fell over. I didn't drag him down on purpose, Carlos, so you can take that look off your face. It was an accident!'

'Of course,' he agreed blandly. 'And earlier?' he persisted.

'He was cross because I was late back,' she said non-committally. Then trying to sound casual, she asked, 'Who's Eleanor? A friend of the family?'

'No, well, yes, sort of,' he said hesitantly. 'Her father is on the vine growers board; he hopes Adriao will offer for her.'

'Offer for her?' she asked faintly.

'*Sim*. It is time Adriao was married, and she is very suitable, good background, wealthy...' With a wry shrug, he continued smoothly, 'It would be a good match.'

'I see,' she murmured weakly. 'Adriao didn't say... Well, there's no reason why he should, of course...'

'No. She has been staying in Lisbon with relatives... You need a drink,' he said decisively. Getting to his feet, he went across to the bar. 'What will you have, Kate? Gin and tonic?'

'Yes, thank you, that will be fine.' Adriao married? And yet why should she be surprised? He was in his mid-thirties, surprising really that he hadn't married before this. 'She looks very young,' she commented as she automatically accepted her drink.

'Nineteen.'

'Gentle, and nervous—biddable...'

'Yes.'

'Everything I'm not,' she murmured, then waved her hand limply to negate her words. Why on earth had she said that? Forcing a grin, she saluted Carlos with her glass. 'Thanks. Sorry about the shrubs.'

'Shrubs can be replaced.' With another rather speculative look, which Kate fortunately didn't see, Carlos poured himself a glass of wine, before adding quietly, 'I'm sorry.'

'Sorry?' she asked, bewildered. 'Why should you be sorry? It was my fault for being so damned clumsy.' Only she had the feeling they were discussing different subjects. Narrowing her eyes on the bland face opposite, she said softly, 'Trying to tell me something, Carlos?'

'Me? Good heavens, no. What should I be trying to tell you, Kate?'

'I have no idea.' Her face thoughtful, a shred of amusement returning to her lovely eyes, she finished her drink. 'I think I'll go to bed.' Replacing her glass on the bar, she gave a mocking little wave. 'Goodnight, Carlos.'

'Goodnight, Kate.'

Walking slowly and rather unhappily up to her room, she tried to work out what the devil Carlos was up to. He was up to something. Manipulation? But why? And why had Adriao been so mad? Slamming his glass on the bar like that. Maybe it had something to do with seeing Eleanor again, although why that should annoy him, she couldn't imagine, but talk about chalk and cheese, she mused as she pushed open her bedroom door. Poor Eleanor, there was definitely a touch of the lamb to the slaughter there. And what business is it of yours, Kate Lassiter? None. Only the thought of Adriao with Eleanor, of that strong, carved face bending towards the young girl as he kissed her goodnight, made her ache inside. Conjuring up an image of his face as he had stood, pressed close against her, in the garden, she shivered. He'd looked—what, Kate? she asked herself impatiently. How had he looked? Tense, angry, hating her almost? With another little shiver, she determinedly tried to banish both Adriao and Eleanor from her mind. It was time she got on with the reason for her being in Portugal, never mind the personal problems of her reluctant host. And it might not be a bad idea to get away from him for a few days before they ended up in another war. Because she didn't want another war. She wanted him to love her. A startled expression crossing her face, she froze, her hand arrested halfway to the light switch. Oh, no, Kate, she told herself forcefully. Oh, no. Don't let's be stupid about this!

Finally snapping down the light switch with an abrupt, almost angry gesture as though light would dispel her thoughts, she walked swiftly across to the bathroom and closed the door with a firm little click. No more, Kate. Most definitely no more! That way lay the sort of heartache she'd never be able to cope with. And it wasn't true! Why on earth would she want him to love her? She didn't even like him!

After a night spent tossing and turning, being pursued by an angry Adriao, she got up far too early and gave herself a severe talking to. He doesn't like you. He won't ever like you, so no more, Kate. You have to think about the article, and only the article, which means travelling around, seeing the countryside, the towns. Right. Packing a few things in a large leather bag, she left it in the hall while she went to have breakfast with Carlos.

'You're up bright and early,' he said with a smile as she joined him.

'Mmm, I thought I'd go off exploring, get started on the article,' she explained, her face and voice determined. 'What?' she asked, puzzled, when he looked distinctly worried.

'Er——'

'Oh, come on, Carlos. You're not worried about what Adriao will say, are you?'

'What? No, no, not Adriao, but I was just trying to think of a polite way of enquiring when you would be back?'

'Oh.' She smiled. 'I don't know, a few days, maybe . . . No?' she asked comically when he shook his head. 'Not a few days?'

'Well, yes, certainly a few days,' he agreed awkwardly. 'But each night you must be here.'

'I must?' she asked, confused.

'*Sim*. Because of the rules . . .'

'Oh, good grief,' she exclaimed in disgust. 'I'd forgotten all about that damned race. Do I really have to be here each night?'

'Yes, I am afraid so, Kate. It is difficult for you?'

'Well, of course it's difficult for me!'

'Could you not visit the nearer places first? Then, when Peter arrives . . .'

Making a little tutting noise in the back of her throat, she then grinned to show it wasn't directed at him. 'When is Peter coming? Have you heard from him?'

'Yes, of course, he'll be here in a few days, I think.'

'Oh, all right, if I must, I must.'

'Thank you,' he said happily now that he'd got his own way. 'And you don't need to worry about seeing Adriao,' he murmured blandly. 'He's gone to Lisbon for a few days.'

'Who said I was worried about seeing him?' she asked offhandedly.

'No one, of course. You will be careful, won't you?'

'Yes, Carlos, I will be careful.' Getting to her feet, she dropped a light kiss on his cheek. 'I'll even be back before it gets dark.'

How much had the wretch Carlos seen in her face? He must have seen something else he wouldn't have made that crack about her not seeing Adriao. Oh, Kate, why can't you manage your life the way others do?

* * *

For the next few days, she toured round the nearby towns, always keeping her promise to be back at the castle before dark, and if her thoughts dwelled more often than they should on Adriao and the fair Eleanor, then they were no one's business but her own.

It was certainly a land of contrasts, she discovered, a harsh land, perhaps, yet with a friendly feel, a warmth that was due only in part to the weather, and, slowly, without Adriao's disturbing presence, and, thankfully, no more cracks from Carlos, she began to relax, enjoy herself. She left the nearest of the large towns until last—Porto, and, out of curiosity, and only curiosity, she told herself, she located the Palace Hotel. The hotel she should have been staying at, would have been staying at, if it hadn't been for Peter's wretched machinations. Walking into Reception, she returned outside a few minutes later with a frown in her lovely eyes. Before returning to the car, she walked slowly round the town, had a look in the shops, then made her way to the central park, her thoughts preoccupied. Perching on one of the wooden benches, she stared blindly before her. She saw nothing of the people walking leisurely past, the obvious tourists with their cameras and maps, saw only the puzzled face of the reception clerk in the hotel.

Eventually recalling herself to the time, she glanced at her watch, and, seeing it was gone five, she returned to the car and slowly negotiated her way across the busy town and back to the main road.

When she reached the castle, hot, sticky and tired, she decided to write up some of her notes while they were still fresh in her mind before going to have a shower. Accepting with a smile the long, cold drink one of the servants brought her, she put her feet up on the veranda rail, her pad on her knee, her drink beside her. Hearing footsteps, knowing without even looking that it was Adriao, she tensed and turned her head warily. This was the first time they had met since the incident in the garden and she wasn't sure how to behave, then had her thoughts diverted as she realised how tired he looked. What had he been up to in her absence? Too much heavy petting? she wondered, a trifle cynically. Deliberately fostering her dislike to cover her feelings of inadequacy, she murmured politely, if a trifle stiffly, 'Adriao.'

'Katherine,' he intoned formally.

'You look tired,' she commented without conscious thought.

'Do I?' he asked non-committally.

'Mmm. How's the fair Eleanor?' she continued. For some reason she couldn't even begin to explain to herself, she wanted to goad him, ruffle that cool exterior he'd encased himself in.

'We will leave Eleanor out of our discussions, thank you,' he informed her coldly.

'Why?'

'Because she's none of your business.'

'True. Do you love her?'

'That also is none of your business.'

'Meaning you don't.'

'Meaning we have liking, respect,' he listed, a slight edge creeping into his voice, 'and, unlike you, my dear Kate, she is pure, biddable——'

'Boring . . .'

'She would make me a good wife,' he continued, his jaw beginning to clench. 'She would grace my home, my table——'

'Your bed . . .'

'And my bed,' he confirmed, dipping his head in an arctic little acknowledgement. 'Or is that what this is all about, Kate? You wish to take her place?'

'No, Adriao, I do not wish to take her place,' she denied hastily as she felt an alarming dip in her stomach at the very thought of it.

Having lost that round she instigated another one, one she was much surer of winning. 'I went into Porto today,' she began mildly.

'Did you?'

'Yes, to the Palace Hotel. And I thought, while I was there, I ought perhaps to apologise for not turning up to claim my room...' When he didn't respond, merely looked at her, his dark eyes expressionless, she persevered, 'Guess what?'

'I have no idea.'

'They hadn't re-let my room after all.'

'Had they not?' he queried politely.

'No. Odd, that, don't you think?'

'Extremely.'

'Adriao!' she snapped in exasperation. 'You told me they hadn't kept it!'

'So I did.'

'Well, why?' she demanded.

'Presumably, my dear Kate, a mere misunderstanding. On my part of course.' Holding her mutinous eyes for long moments, he asked blandly, 'So how have you been getting on with your research?'

'Oh, fine,' she said sarcastically. 'I've been having a wow of a time!'

'I'm so glad.' Turning his back, he leaned on the veranda rail and stared out over the sun-warmed valley. 'You have all the information you need?'

'No. There are still one or two things I need to check,' she muttered stiffly.

'Such as?'

'Such as, did Portugal really get its name from the city of Cale being on one bank of the Douro in what is now called Oporto, or Porto, and the port on the other?'

'Yes.'

'Yes what?' she asked irritably.

With a long sigh, which was most definitely meant to be insulting, she decided, and still without looking at her, he recited, 'Oporto simply means the port. The Romans named it Portus Cale, and from that the region between the Douro and Minho became known as Portucale. It formed part of the dowry of Princess Theresa when she married Henri of Burgundy in, oh, 1095, I think, and it was under his son that the country gained its freedom and independence from the Moors and took its name from this region of Portucale.'

'Thank you,' she said tersely.

'You're welcome. What else?'

'Braga. I found a reference that it's claimed to be the capital of the Minho. Is it?'

'For sure. People claim all sorts of things, who will refute it? It was originally an important Roman town named Bacara Augusta. It was taken by the Suabi when they invaded the area, then by the Visigoths and the Moors. It was liberated by King Ferdinand of Leon and became the seat of the Archbishops. They were said to have more importance than the Kings. There are all sorts of books on the major towns in the library, the room behind my study. You are welcome to go in there any time you wish.'

'Thank you, I might just as well, mightn't I?' she asked waspishly. 'It couldn't be any more text-like than what you've just spouted at me!' Slamming her glass down, she got to her feet, intending to go indoors and up to her room.

'Kate?' he called softly as she reached the edge of the terrace.

'What?'

'You will be ready at nine tomorrow morning. I have made arrangements for you to visit the wine caves.'

'Oh, have you? Well, now you can go and unmake them!' she retorted rudely. 'I've already made plans for tomorrow!' Stomping inside and up to her room, she slammed the bedroom door to relieve her feelings. Damned autocrat! Talking to Adriao was like trying to hold a conversation with a shop mannequin! And he thoroughly routed you, didn't he? That was what rankled! Well, tomorrow she would go and book herself back in the hotel in Porto and to hell with the blasted race rules!

Still feeling ruffled and confused and out of her depth, she stalked into the bathroom. Carlos had asked if she deliberately goaded Adriao in order to get a reaction, and she'd denied it. Only he'd been right, hadn't he? She was behaving like the spoilt child Adriao had once accused her of being. Not liking herself very much, she reached miserably out to turn on the shower—nothing happened. Oh, no. Oh, please don't do this to me. Closing her eyes, she took a deep breath and tried again. Nothing. With a despairing sigh, she wrapped a towel round herself and walked across to the bedroom door. Opening it, she peered out, hoping to see the little maid Maria who had been on the landing a few minutes ago.

'Maria?' she called softly, and, when the maid's head appeared out of another door further along, she beckoned. Taking her into the bathroom, she demonstrated the lack of water. With much tutting and clicking of levers, Maria sighed, then looked thoughtful. Grasping Kate's hand, she practically dragged her along the corridor and into another bedroom. Tugging her across the room, she opened the bathroom door and tried that shower. Cool water sprayed efficiently out. Beaming, Maria indicated for her to use this one.

'Whose room is it?' Kate asked slowly, and was answered with an incomprehensible flood of Portuguese, not one word of which she understood. Shrugging, she dropped the towel, and stepped under the shower, and Maria went back to whatever it was she'd been doing.

She didn't know what alerted her, a feeling of being watched perhaps, but, whatever it was, the prickling feeling wouldn't go away. Turning off the shower, she listened, then turned her head. Adriao was standing not two feet away, his feet bare, his shirt already un-buttoned, and half off one shoulder. He was watching her, his face completely devoid of expression. With a yell of alarm, she grabbed the towel to cover herself, stepped too quickly from the shower, and slipped on the wet tiled floor.

'Don't touch me!' she screeched as he took a step forward.

'Why should I wish to touch you?' he asked with insulting distaste as he finished removing his shirt. 'I was merely going to turn the shower back on.'

Glaring at him, feeling stupid and furious, she struggled to rise and keep the towel in place all at the same time.

'Is this the best you can do?' he asked smoothly as he tossed his shirt on to the edge of the laundry basket.

'What?' she asked blankly.

'This seduction scene, is it the best you could think of? First the deliberate attempt to anger me, and, when that didn't work, this. Don't like being ignored, do you, Kate? Can't cope with indifference.' And, because his words confirmed much of what she had been thinking, she flushed guiltily, and hated herself for doing so, and hated him for being unkind enough to mention it.

'So, are you ready now?' he continued. His voice might be mild, his face bland, but he was very, very angry.

'If you mean by that cryptic remark have I finished showering,' she said through her teeth, 'then yes, I have!'

'Splendid.' With a smile that Kate decided she didn't like very much, he began walking carefully towards her.

'What the hell do you think you're doing?'

'Evicting you from my room?' he asked softly, dangerously.

'You don't need to evict me! I can walk quite easily on my own two feet!'

'But not fast enough, and if you'd any sort of sense at all you would have run the moment you saw me. You didn't—and we both know why, don't we?'

'No, we bloody don't! And take your damned hands off me!' she yelled, her voice rising to a high squeak as warm palms descended to her rigid shoulders. 'I told you I don't like being touched!'

'Then you shouldn't have come into my room— and I am getting a little tired of being treated as a no-account peasant that you can wind up and put down at your whim,' he concluded as he easily picked her up and threw her over one shoulder. His movements were smooth, controlled, and would presumably have worked very well if the floor hadn't been wet. If Adriao hadn't had bare feet. As it was, he stepped on the same patch of wet floor that had been Kate's undoing, lost his balance, tried to save both her and himself, and saved neither.

Crushed beneath him on the cold tiled floor, the towel gone, she stared up at his grim face, shocked and incapable of movement. She was aware with the part of her brain that wasn't frozen that her breasts were crushed against his naked chest, that her thighs were trapped beneath his and that his brown eyes had slowly darkened to black. 'No,' she began on a snatched, panicky breath as his mouth captured hers with a savage swoop.

It was an assault of anger, frustration and hatred, of himself as much as her, but by no stretch of the imagination could it be called a kiss. It was a degradation to both of them. And it stirred something in both of them they'd be unable to forget. He ground his mouth against hers as though she was something foul he must conquer, and, to her everlasting shame, she responded with a violence that matched his own. Holding him, her palms warm against his naked back, she moved beneath him, parted her mouth eagerly.

When she gave an involuntary groan of desire and frustration, he lifted his head with a jerky little movement and stared down at her, his face a mask, devoid of any expression at all.

For such a long time he just stared at her, until, finally, he said flatly, 'So now you know.'

Her eyes wide and shocked, she gazed back at him until the words finally penetrated. So now she knew. Wanting to scream a denial, shocked disbelief held her rigid. Releasing her breath in a jerky little puff, she frantically shook her head, her eyes wide and frightened. 'No,' she whispered through numb lips. 'No. No!' she yelled. Galvanised into action, she thrust him away, struggled to her feet, grabbed frantically at the towel and fled. No, her mind insisted as she ran along the corridor to her room. No. As she reached her door, she heard his own slam violently shut and she winced. Shaking uncontrollably, it took her a few moments to be able to twist the knob to open her door, then she fell thankfully inside.

Feeling vulnerable and exposed with only the towel to cover her, she hastily dragged on underwear, loose cotton trousers and a T-shirt, her wet hair soaking the neck and shoulders in seconds.

Her eyes still wide with shock, her mind blank, her hands trembling, she rubbed her hair dry then quickly brushed it flat. She couldn't stay. She must leave now—then she swung round in alarm as the door opened and Adriao stood framed in the entrance— dressed only as he had been a few minutes earlier, his tanned chest still bare. Backing up against the dressing-table, her hands clenched on the top, she stared at him. 'Get out of here,' she said shakily, her eyes wide and frightened.

'No. We have to talk.' Stepping inside, he closed the door behind him.

'No, we don't!'

'Kate, calm down, we——'

'No! You're mad,' she whispered as he took a step forward.

'*Sim,'* he agreed softly.

'Why?' she asked in bewilderment. 'Why did you do it?'

'You know why.'

'I don't.' Looking bewildered, and very, very vulnerable, she just stared at him, her beautiful eyes filled with confusion.

'Yes, you do. Always so busy fighting, aren't you, Kate? Always so busy being right,' he murmured, confusing her more. 'Why were you in my shower?' he demanded softly.

'Well, it wasn't an invitation!' she snapped huskily, her voice shaking. 'Mine wouldn't work and Maria dragged me in there!'

'I see.'

'Good! Now get out of here!'

Surprisingly, he did. Just turned, opened the door, and left. Staring in even more confusion at the closed door, she didn't relax until she heard his footsteps retreat down the corridor, then let out her breath on a long, shaky sigh. She couldn't face him again. Couldn't face the knowledge she would see in his eyes, that she had responded. That his punishment, his violence, his anger, had not subdued her—but excited her. She didn't think she could live with her own knowledge of it either. In all her twenty-four years she'd strongly denied having any feelings for the opposite sex, that she had ever been attracted to a man—because she was afraid that those feelings would never be reciprocated. There, she'd admitted it—yet instead of feeling relief, she wanted to weep. All those years of sexual repression—and she had to respond to violence. And for making her acknowledge the truth about herself she thought she hated him.

Collapsing down on to the edge of the bed she put her face in her hands. A psychologist would have had a field day, she thought bitterly. He could blame her upbringing, her parents, and in part he would be right—but not entirely. A lot of it could be put down to her own cowardice. Her fear of rejection. Her fear of putting feelings to the test. Her father had blamed her for her mother's defection; he'd told her she was unfeeling, unlovable, plain, and uninteresting. Her mother had pitied her—when she remembered she was there, had instilled within her the knowledge that she would never be sure if people ever liked her for herself, or for her money. And subsequent events had often proved her right.

Her mother's boyfriends had treated her as though she didn't exist, as though she was a nonentity—until she had come into her inheritance, when, suddenly, she had become flavour of the month. And she'd allowed them all to get away with it, allowed them to colour her behaviour—and for that she was a fool. Even now, with both of them dead, their legacy remained. She'd placed herself very firmly behind her own personal wall and defied anyone to broach it. It had not occurred to her that she might one day want to broach it herself.

So now you know, he'd said. Yes, so now she knew. It hadn't been dislike, hatred, contempt, she'd felt for him, a need to be acknowledged as a person, but naked, unacknowledged desire that had shredded already raw nerves, distorted her reasoning. Perhaps that was what she had subconsciously been denying all these years, the fear that she was like her mother. A woman with an unfulfilled, or unfulfillable, sexual appetite. If you never have it, you'll never miss it— and never want it. Is that what she'd subconsciously thought? Unless someone like Adriao came along and woke the beast.

With a long, deep sigh, she lowered her hands and got to her feet. Concentrating on the task in hand, she repacked her holdall with clean clothes, rammed everything else into her suitcases and left them beside the wardrobe. She would come back for them when she'd made sure she could get a room at the Palace Hotel in Porto, then she'd finish writing her article, and, as soon as her car was ready, go home, back to England, and safety.

With her bag slung over one shoulder, her holdall in her hand, she opened the door and hurried downstairs. With her hand on the front door, she froze as a familiar voice drawled from behind her, 'Well, well, well, and where are you off to in such an all-fired hurry, my little friend?'

Swinging round, she stared into the grinning face of Peter. Took in, without seeing, the fair hair that fell boyishly over his forehead, the glass he held in one hand. Her eyes still wide with her anguish, her mind determinedly refusing to grasp anything but what had just happened, she stared at him blankly.

'Kate?' he asked softly, his face sobering, his blue eyes worried. 'What's wrong?'

'Nothing,' she denied jerkily. 'I'm going away for a few days. The article . . .'

'But I've only just arrived.'

'I know. I—er—have to go.' Hearing a sound from upstairs and terrified that it was Adriao, she yanked open the front door and escaped.

'Kate!'

Not even daring to hesitate, she climbed quickly behind the wheel and drove away. She'd explain to Peter later, or make an excuse, or something. Only not now.

Trying desperately to banish everything that had happened, she concentrated on her driving, only to find that her mind went its own way regardless. She felt demeaned. Anger warring with guilt and confusion, she drove mindlessly as she repeatedly played the hateful scene over and over in her head, and it was some time before she took in her surroundings, only to discover that she hadn't the faintest idea where she was. Well, it didn't matter, did it? Didn't matter where she went so long as it was as far away from the *castelo* as possible.

Stopping in the first big town she came to, the spa town Vidago, she found herself a room in a little hotel tucked away in a side-street.

With a great deal of determination, she ruthlessly pushed Adriao and her own behaviour to the back of her mind and began cobbling her article together. The sooner it was finished, the sooner she could return to England—only the far too vivid recollections refused to be banished. As soon as her concentration lapsed, it was there, back in the forefront of her mind, the feel of his mouth on hers. His tongue against hers, the warmth and strength of him—and then his look that had been so completely without expression. Insultingly so. Hating herself and him, she fought to regain a sense of proportion.

She stayed two days in the town, blanking out everything but the article. It wasn't as good as it should have been, but the best she could do in the circumstances, and when she returned to the *castelo* she would pick up her suitcases, find out about her car, and leave.

With luck, she'd be able to sneak in, have a quick word with Peter, and get out again without having to see Adriao. Deliberately delaying her arrival until it was dark, she drove into the courtyard, and then just stared around her in dismay. There were at least five cars parked there, barely leaving room for her own estate. Tempted to go away and come back later, she then condemned herself for her cowardice. All she had to do was go inside, collect her suitcases and leave. She didn't even have to see Peter. He would understand when she explained later, back home. And she could write to Carlos, thank him for his kindness... Having settled it to her satisfaction, she took a deep breath, got out of the car and walked inside—and came to a shocked halt. There were people everywhere! The race drivers, she discovered, and, before she could get halfway up the stairs to her room, nodding and excusing herself every foot of the way, Carlos spotted her.

'Kate! Come and meet everybody!'

'No, Carlos,' she began firmly. Then, finding she didn't quite have the courage to blurt out to him that she was merely there to collect her suitcases, she prevaricated, 'I'm hot, sticky, and, to be honest, in no mood to meet a lot of strangers...'

'You look fine,' he argued, obviously in one of his 'I'm not to be thwarted' moods, and, before she could continue her ascent, he'd nipped up beside her, taken her bag from her nerveless fingers, and escorted her back down again. 'Come.'

'Carlos,' she protested, 'I'm not very good with people I don't know...' Only she might just as well have saved her breath; he took not a blind bit of notice and without being unbearably rude and shrugging him off she had no choice but to go with him.

Dropping her bag at the foot of the stairs, he ushered her out to the terrace.

If she hadn't felt so awkward and terrified of meeting Adriao again, she would probably have found the whole thing amusing. There were the six Portuguese drivers, excluding Adriao, plus their foreign co-drivers, who hardly filled the *castelo* to capacity, yet every room she went into seemed full of people, laughing, chatting, offering her drinks, which she didn't want. They were friendly and kind, most of them with a smattering of English, flattering and flirtatious, especially the French driver, Marcel, who trapped her up against the wall and wouldn't let her go until Carlos kindly rescued her, and through it all Adriao's expressionless face followed her. He presumably thought she was trying to exert her supposed charms on his friends, which was no doubt why he kept trying to head her off and get her alone so that he could castigate her further, she decided, deliberately whipping up her anger so that she would be able to cope with him when he did manage to corner her. Which he would, she knew. Adriao was nothing if not determined.

Fortunately, every time he nearly succeeded in cornering her, someone thwarted him. And, even if there hadn't been anyone else to do so, she'd have done her utmost to thwart him herself. And, even more irritating, every time she caught a glimpse of Peter's fair head and tried to follow him, he disappeared. If she hadn't known better, she would have thought he was avoiding her.

Eventually, of course, everyone had to go home and before she could escape to her room Adriao managed to finally trap her on the terrace, and one look at his face convinced her that running away would do no good at all. He looked arrogant and haughty, lord of all he surveyed. Well, she might be a nobody, but that didn't give him the right to look down on her. Her chin tilted, she glared at him.

'Think you could avoid me forever?' he asked softly.

'One lives in hope,' she retorted flippantly. 'And what did you expect? A warm smile? Now get out of my way, I'm tired. I'm going up to my room and——'

'We need to talk——'

'No, we don't,' she denied furiously. 'We have nothing to talk about. I'm going up to collect my suitcase, and then I'm leaving. I'll let you know where I am when I've found somewhere to stay so that you can tell the garage.' As she went to brush past him, he caught her elbow in a firm grip and pushed her none too gently into a chair.

Standing in front of her, arms folded, legs apart, he said quietly, 'You think running away will solve all your problems?'

'It might. At least it would take me out of your orbit.'

'No, it wouldn't,' he denied, his voice still quiet, serious. 'It would just mean I'd have to follow you.'

'Why would it?'

'Because we wouldn't have had our talk—and we need to. You are all right?'

'Of course,' she said stiffly. 'Is there any reason why I shouldn't be?'

'No,' he said with unexpected gentleness. 'Why so angry, Kate? Is it really so terrible to be wanted? Oh, I know I should not have behaved so, and, believe me, I regret it very much, but I am only human, and seeing you in my shower, naked . . .' Then, as though angry with himself, he swung away, his hands resting on the rail as he stared out over the valley. 'You made me angry . . .'

'Oh, I see, so it's my fault,' she said icily, 'and that makes it all right to insult me.'

'No! I thought——'

'I know what you thought, Adriao. You made your feelings perfectly clear.' Getting once more to her feet, she faced him defiantly. 'Goodbye, Adriao.'

'Kate?' he called as she reached the door, and when she swung back, a look of almost desperation in her eyes, he made an uncharacteristic gesture of uncertainty. 'Before you go, there is something I would like you to see.'

'What? Your etchings?' she asked sarcastically, to hide her hurt.

'No, Kate, a photograph—and that remark was not worthy of you. Come.' Holding out his hand to her, he sighed when she childishly put both hands behind her back. Turning, he led the way inside. Going across to the bureau in the corner, he pulled open the top drawer and took out a framed photograph. Staring down at it for a moment, he then handed it to her.

Reluctantly taking it from him, she glanced down. It was a photograph of a young woman, a very beautiful young woman. Without the faintest idea what sort of response was required of her, she looked up. 'So?'

'She does not remind you of anyone?' he asked quietly.

'No.'

Turning back to the bureau, he took another, smaller photograph from the drawer and handed it to her. A coloured photograph. It was of the same woman, only this time Kate could see that her eyes were a startling purple-blue, amethyst almost, like her own.

'Her name is Candida,' Adriao explained quietly.

'And?'

'And she was to have been my wife.'

'Was?' she queried, confused.

'*Sim*. Was. She chose someone else.'

'I see,' she said flatly. Staring at his proud, autocratic face, she thought she saw very well. It must have given his pride one hell of a battering to have the woman he had magnanimously selected choose someone else. A man like him, with his long line of illustrious forebears, wouldn't take very kindly to being jilted, would he? 'I'm sorry,' she said inadequately, 'but I really don't see what it has to do with me.'

'Don't you, Kate?' Removing the photographs from her lax grasp, he returned them to the drawer and closed it quietly. Then, pushing his hands into the pockets of his grey trousers, he turned to face her. 'Before we met, both Peter and Isabella had talked about you, about their friend Kate. I had, of course, seen the newspaper articles, but I did not know you, so naturally I did not have an opinion one way or another—until you came into the agency. I was angry that day, Peter and I had been arguing about the article. I was feeling impatient, railroaded, and then the door opened, I turned, annoyed at the interruption, to find you glaring at me——'

'You glared at me first,' she argued, then lapsed into silence at his gesture of irritation.

'You looked at me with such defiance, as though challenging me, and it was as if Candida had come back to taunt me. It was such a shock, Kate, to be reminded so suddenly of something I had wished to forget. You were arrogant and aggressive, and——'

'I was arrogant?' she exclaimed in disbelief. '*I* was?'

Looking at her, he gave a small, twisted smile. 'All right, we both were; now please, Kate, let me finish, hmm? I think perhaps I wasn't used to being treated with such contempt,' he continued with a small frown, as though even he wasn't sure that his explanation was the right one. 'If I had not been in a temper that day, who knows? But, whatever the reason, it all seemed to get out of hand. Each time we met, it was worse. The more dismissive I was towards you, the more arrogant and argumentative you became. If you had remained quiet, dignified, perhaps I would not have behaved as I did. I do not know,' he confessed. 'It does not excuse my behaviour, but I hoped an explanation might make you at least understand it.'

'Yes,' she said lamely. And it did, she supposed. It also explained why Carlos had looked so surprised the first time they'd met. It did not, however, explain his amusement. He surely couldn't find it in the least funny that a young woman who looked a little like his nephew's one-time fiancée had come to stay at the *castelo*.

'Sometimes, I thought you must know, your behaviour, your taunts...'

'How could I know?' she exclaimed.

'I thought perhaps Carlos might have told you.'

'No. He looked somewhat surprised when he first saw me, but no, he didn't explain. Only what I don't understand is why he seems to find the whole thing amusing.'

'Because, apart from the colour of your eyes, and the defiant way you glare at me, you are the complete antithesis of Candida.'

'So what's so amusing about that?' she asked in confusion.

Sighing, he looked down and stared at his feet for long moments before glancing up. His face was empty, she saw, his eyes bleak, and yet nothing would ever take away that look of superiority he so unconsciously wore, even if he was about to air his dirty washing in public. 'I will begin at the beginning,' he said flatly. 'The marriage was an arrangement, as is often the case between old families. An accepted part of everyday living. I neither liked nor disliked her when we met. It is perhaps hard for you to understand, but that is how it is. Most marriages of that kind are happy enough, and all would presumably have been well if Candida had not discovered her hatred of the countryside. She hated the isolation, the roads, the people, everything it was possible to hate, Candida hated. Only she did not say so, not in words. Candida was given to martyred silences, sighs, glances of abject misery.' Taking a deep breath, centuries of pride settling on his strong face, he continued stiffly, 'She also hated what she referred to as my animal instincts. She was reared in a household where a peck on the cheek was considered forward. Where procreation took place in a darkened room between the sheets. A duty, rather than a pleasure. In short, I frightened the life out of her. None of which would have stopped her marrying me, of course,' he pointed out cynically, 'because I was wealthy, well connected, and if she had not met someone wealthier and even better connected, then the marriage would have gone ahead. Only she did meet him, he also had the advantage of being older, a great deal older——'

'And presumably older men do not have the sexual drive of someone younger,' she put in bluntly.

'*Sim,*' he agreed, 'I am sure that is a consideration Candida took into account.'

You're hating this, aren't you? she asked him silently as she searched his dark, empty eyes. To someone with your pride, it is a slur on your good name, and, much as she disliked his arrogance, she didn't want him humbled in this way. 'You don't have to tell me,' she said hesitantly.

His eyes registering his surprise, he said haughtily, 'Of course I do not have to. It is my choice.'

Staring at him, she gave a small, wry smile. 'Oh, Adriao,' she exclaimed softly, then motioned him to go on.

'I could perhaps have forgiven her had she explained to me personally, only she did not. She did not have the courage to face me, nor to write. She wrote to her mother, who was incapable of keeping anything to herself, regardless of how private it might be, something Candida knew very well.'

And so she made him a laughing-stock. Dear lord, what a cruel thing to do. 'Where is she now?' she asked quietly.

'In Lisbon,' he said dismissively.

'And is that where you've just been? To see her?'

'To see her?' he echoed, a flicker of arrogant astonishment crossing his face. 'Why would I wish to see her?'

'I have no idea,' she admitted with a heavy sigh. 'But none of that explains why Carlos thinks it amusing.'

'I am not used to being argued with,' he explained aloofly, 'and it amused Carlos to see you do so. He thinks my pride a foolish thing and that an aggressive little spitfire poking holes in it will do me the world of good.'

'Only, of course, it doesn't,' she said stiffly, any compassion she might have felt rapidly disappearing. 'It only makes you worse.'

'*Sim,* until I lost my temper, and my reason, and admitted to myself that my feelings for you had nothing whatever to do with Candida. I fought you

and insulted you and told myself it was justified because you were a blackmailing little tramp—because
I needed to believe that—until I found you naked in
my shower, and behaved like the animal Candida
always accused me of being.'

'So now you know,' she whispered. He hadn't been
talking about her, but about himself. In that one
moment she had been the Candida he had always
wanted to punish. All he had seen was naked flesh
and amethyst eyes and reason had been left by the
wayside. Had he loved her, his Candida? Despite his
explanation that it was an arranged match, had he
loved her? And had it hurt *him*, not his pride, that
she had not loved him back? Which would account
for his treating her the way she tended to treat all men.
One rejection and you tended to treat everyone the
same. Well, she could understand that.

'I am sorry, Kate.'

With a funny little shrug, she looked away. 'It
doesn't matter.' But it did, it mattered too damned
much. Turning away so that he couldn't see her face,
she walked back out to the terrace. She had known
he didn't like her, didn't see her as a person, or not
a nice person anyway, and, although she had been
angry and hurt by his behaviour in the bathroom, she
had at least thought it was her body he had wanted.
Only it wasn't. It had been Candida's.

Staring up at the dark sky, her eyes bleak, she
sighed. Hearing his footsteps behind her, she turned
and leaned against the rail.

'There was a phone call for you while you were
away,' he informed her quietly. 'Someone called
Jackie. Apparently Peter gave her my number. She
asked me to tell you that Christopher had been taken

into hospital, but that he was all right. She thought you'd want to know. Who is Christopher?'

'A friend,' she said simply.

'I see. Just a friend, Kate? Or more?'

And because she was hurting, and because she needed to keep some pride, she said quietly, 'More. I love him. Very much.' And so she did. He was five years old and suffered from cerebral palsy. 'I'll give Jackie a ring in the morning, if I may.'

'Of course.'

'Thank you.'

When the silence stretched on too long, she pushed herself away from the rail with the intention of going upstairs, and then suddenly remembered Peter. She'd forgotten all about her need to see him. Halting, she turned back. 'Speaking of Peter,' she said quietly, 'where is he? Every time I nearly caught up with him earlier, he disappeared——'

'Gone!' Carlos said dramatically from behind her.

'What?' she asked, swinging round in shock.

'Gone,' he repeated.

'Carlos,' she exclaimed impatiently, 'don't keep saying that! Gone where?'

'Home.'

'But he was here, I saw him.'

'Yes, but he was not feeling very well.'

'Then why didn't he say so? Why keep avoiding me?'

With a long, tragic sigh, he spread his hands and explained forlornly, 'Chicken-pox.'

'Chicken-pox? Don't be ridiculous! He's forty-six! You don't get chicken-pox at forty-six!'

'You don't?' he queried comically.

'Carlos!' she said through her teeth. 'Stop playing games! Where is Peter?'

'But I told you, Kate. He has gone home. Vitor kindly ran him to the airport because he thought he had chicken-pox. Apparently one of his girls at the agency had it, and he was afraid he'd caught it.'

Staring at him, she shook her head weakly. 'No,' she whispered. 'I don't believe it.' Turning to look at Adriao, she asked hesitantly, 'Did you know?'

Returning her stare, he briefly flicked his eyes towards his uncle, then shook his head, and she had the absurd notion that he was suddenly trying very hard not to laugh.

'Chicken-pox?' he queried, his voice stifled.

'Yes! Chicken-pox!' Carlos said forcefully. 'He didn't want to give it to anyone else, so he has gone home! And both of you,' he continued impatiently, 'are entirely missing the point! It doesn't matter what illness he has! It is sufficient that he has one!'

'It is?'

'Oh, may the dear lord give me patience,' he exclaimed. 'Think! If he's ill, he won't be able to take part in the race! Adriao! Will you please pay attention?'

'Sorry,' he muttered, his voice most definitely quivering, and Kate swung round to glare at him.

'It isn't funny!' she snapped.

'No, Kate,' he agreed placatingly. 'Of course it is not funny.' Straightening attentively, he asked his uncle, 'So what do we do now?'

'Find someone else, obviously.'

'In one week?'

'Yes! In one week!'

'*Deus,*' Adriao exclaimed. Taking a step forward to face his uncle, and momentarily blocking Kate's view of him, he remained silent for long moments, then turned away, his shoulders slightly hunched as he began to range up and down the terrace throwing names at Carlos as he did so, every one of which Carlos rejected. 'Well, what about that English friend of Joao's?'

'He's in Canada!'

'Hmm. Well, what about Vitor's brother-in-law? What's his name? He's English, isn't he?'

'No, American.'

'Does he have to be English?' Kate asked quietly, still thoroughly bewildered by the whole turn of events. And why did she keep getting the feeling that Adriao's whole behaviour was an act?

'Yes,' Carlos said absently.

'Well, maybe Peter hasn't got chicken-pox,' she offered tentatively. 'He might be better in time. I mean, he looked all right when I saw him.'

'Well, he didn't when he left!' Carlos snapped. 'Oh, Kate, I'm sorry,' he apologised. 'It is unforgivable to take my frustration out on you. I'm sure he will be all right, he will have Isabella to nurse him, although I doubt he will make a good patient.'

'Never mind Peter!' Adriao exclaimed, coming to a halt. 'What do we do about a driver? Who else can we——?' Breaking off, he swung round on Kate.

'Oh, no,' she said hastily, backing away. 'Oh, no. Don't look at me!'

'But yes!' Carlos exclaimed. 'It's perfect! Kate's name is already submitted as substitute——'

'I don't care what my name is submitted as!' she said shortly. 'I am not driving in your damned race!'

'But why?' he asked, as though he couldn't possibly have the faintest idea. 'Who else could we get at such short notice?'

'I don't know! Neither do I very much care! But there must be someone!'

'Who? Everyone else is already committed! Besides,' he added with wonderful encouragement, 'it will make a nice finish to your article!'

'Oh, that's really likely to persuade me, isn't it?'

'But it's not difficult—you drive reasonably well, don't you?'

'Reasonably?' she demanded, incensed. 'I'm a damned good driver!'

'Well, there you are, then,' Carlos approved. 'There's no problem.'

'There is every problem!' she said between her teeth. 'I am not going!'

'You can go whichever way you choose,' Carlos continued, deaf and blind to anyone else's problems but his own, or pretending to be. 'You won't have any maps you'll need to decipher. There are check-points, of course, but that's no problem. No outside assistance, but we can work out tentative routes...'

'We?' she asked sweetly.

'Yes! We! If Adriao does not have a co-driver, he cannot go!'

'Shame,' she muttered, still resolutely refusing to look in Adriao's direction, although she knew he was watching her. And if he had the damned nerve to put forward any persuasions she'd tell him just exactly what she thought of him!

'But he has to go!' Carlos continued entreatingly. 'The Ferreira wines must be represented!'

'Then you go! You're bridling with enthusiasm!'

'I'm too old! You think I wouldn't if I could? You have to be between twenty years and fifty!'

'Then you'll just have to find someone else, won't you? Because I—am—not—going!'

# CHAPTER FIVE

WHEN Carlos didn't reply, just continued to regard Kate with a wounded expression, she stamped her foot. 'You're wasting your time, Carlos, I'm not going!'

'But why?'

'You know why!'

'Because of me, Kate?' Adriao asked quietly.

'Of course because of you!' she exclaimed, beginning to feel thoroughly trapped and threatened. 'My God, have you forgotten so soon the drive here?' she demanded. 'We can't be in the same room for five minutes without arguing, let alone a car! It's ridiculous! Carlos,' she appealed, turning to the older man, 'you must see how impossible it will be!'

With a little shrug, and a 'What can I do?' expression, he spread his hands helplessly. 'It has to be you, Kate. There is no one else. Your name was entered.'

'But only because Peter couldn't come!'

'I know, but you can't have more than one substitution.'

'Says who?' she asked scornfully.

'The rules.'

'So show me the rules.'

With a look of sorrow that made her want to hit him, he confessed, 'I do not have a copy here.'

'Oh, really! How convenient! Well, I don't care. I am not going, and that's that! Goodnight, gentlemen!'

Turning on her heel, she stalked off and up to her room. She was not going to be Adriao's co-driver! And in the morning she was leaving, just as she had planned. How in God's name could they expect her to sit in the close confines of a car with a man who destroyed her peace of mind without even looking at her? Because they didn't know... No, that wasn't true. Adriao must know, must have been aware of her violent response in his room, even if he hadn't referred to it, and Carlos certainly knew! She knew he did! She should have gone when she had returned earlier, just collected her suitcases and gone.

Her mind spinning with everything that had happened that evening, it was a long time before she fell asleep, a long time before she calmed down enough to relax. Yet, even with her eyes closed, she could see every expression that had crossed Adriao's face when he had told her about Candida. It had been bad enough being thought a cheat and a blackmailer, but how much worse to be a constant reminder of a woman he had loved.

When she woke, rather later than she intended, she decided to have breakfast before she left. Still determined on her own course of action, she went downstairs and joined both Adriao and his uncle where they sat on the terrace amid the remains of their breakfast. They both smiled at her entrance and got politely to their feet. Carlos's smile was patently false. Adriao's was gentle, concerned almost, which made her heart ache, and she looked hastily away from him. Taking the chair offered in dignified silence, she allowed the little maid to lay her place, then calmly, or as calmly as was possible in the face of two pairs of dark eyes holding exactly the same waiting expression, she buttered her roll and poured herself coffee.

They didn't speak, she didn't speak, just determinedly ate her roll, poured herself fresh coffee and stared aloofly out over the valley. You will not speak first, she adjured herself. You will sit here, calmly, poised and drink your coffee. You will then make a dignified exit and go upstairs, collect your suitcases, and leave. She would not even look at them. She would not look at the purple flowers, the sky, the trees... 'I will not go!' she burst out, calmness and poise fleeing before the storm churning away inside her. 'I won't!'

'No, Kate,' Carlos said calmly, giving her hand an avuncular pat.

'I won't, Carlos,' she warned.

'No, Kate, so you just said. 'I'm sure you're right. You will know your own capabilities best——'

'It's not a question of capabilities!' she yelled. 'I'm perfectly capable! I just—will—not—go!'

With a long, tragic sigh, he turned to his silent nephew. 'We will just have to scratch the Ferreira name,' he said mournfully.

Flinging down her napkin, Kate jumped to her feet. 'It won't work!' she shouted agitatedly. 'I refuse to be made to feel guilty!'

'Oh, Kate,' Carlos admonished as though he'd been cut to the quick, 'how can you even think such a thing? We quite understand your reluctance——'

'No, you don't! Well, yes, you do,' she retorted in exasperation, 'but these tactics will not work!' Storming across to the edge of the terrace, she glared mutinously out over the valley.

'Don't fall off the edge, will you, Kate?' Adriao warned softly and she whirled on him in fury, one arm snaking out to wallop him one.

He wrapped both arms round his head in a defensive gesture that looked utterly ridiculous, as she gritted, 'I hate you!'

His lip quivering, he fought to keep his face blank and failed miserably.

Whirling away, she stormed up to the end of the terrace and indulged in some heavy breathing, her hands wrapped menacingly round the warm wooden support. She wasn't going to give in! She wasn't!

'Who do you think will win now?' Carlos asked quietly.

'Hard to say. Mandel, maybe—pity, that, we had the best car,' Adriao replied, resignation in every level tone.

'Oh, well—didn't you say Kate needed to make a phone call this morning?'

'Yes, and I expect she'll want to ring Isabella to find out how Peter is...'

'May I use the phone?' she gritted.

'Certainly, Kate. Use the one in my study,' Adriao offered kindly. 'It will be more private.'

'Thank you.'

With a wooden expression, she marched indoors and into Adriao's study. She rang Jackie first, her actions stiff and unnatural, her mind still fighting with the battle of the race. Once she'd reassured herself that Christopher was all right, she rang Isabella, who, for some extraordinary reason, seemed to find the whole thing hysterical. 'You will drive instead?' she asked innocently.

'No, I bloody won't!' she yelled, slamming down the phone. 'I am not going to drive!' she announced

to the room at large. 'I refuse to be coerced! Shamed!
Provoked!' Striding round the room, she stared irritably at the pictures on the walls. Original pictures,
she discovered in amazement. A Vélazquez, a
Monet . . .

'Sadly, mine,' Adriao said softly from behind her.
'Not my uncle's.'

'What a pity,' she derided waspishly.

'Poor Kate . . .'

'Don't you poor Kate me, you—you——'

'Wine grower? Race driver? Director of——'

'Oh, shut up!' she said wearily. Staring at him, she
burst out, 'Adriao, you don't want me to drive any
more than I do! You can't! You know what happened
last time!'

'Of course, but, now that we know why, we can
guard against it, can't we?' he asked without a trace
of the previous night's shame at his treatment of her.

'No, we can't. You'll only have to say one word to
provoke me——'

'I could wear a gag——'

'Adriao, be serious!'

'I was,' he protested mildly. 'It will be a simple
matter to fashion one——'

'Adriao!' she exclaimed wrathfully.

With a kind smile that totally infuriated her, he
walked across and placed his hands gently on her
shoulders.

'Don't touch me,' she muttered rebelliously. 'I'm
a substitute, remember?'

'Substitute?' he queried with a frown. 'For Peter,
do you mean?'

'What? No, of course I don't mean for Peter!' she
exclaimed in exasperation. Staring at him, seeing his
confusion, she frowned. Did he really not know what

she meant? Or didn't he think she realised that she'd
been used as a substitute for Candida? Oh, God, why
did things have to get so damned complicated? 'Oh,
I don't know what I mean. Just go away and leave
me alone!'

Keeping her eyes averted and her breathing shallow,
she tried to ignore the feel of his palms on her
shoulders, of the steady rise and fall of the chest in
front of her, of the knowledge that he was watching
her closely.

'Oh, Katie,' he said softly, gently, 'do you really
think me incapable of distinguishing between a dream
and reality?'

Snapping her head round to face him, she said halt-
ingly, 'I don't know what you mean.'

'Yes, you do. You thought I kissed you because I
wanted you to be Candida, didn't you? That I was
substituting you for the need of her. Didn't you?' he
persisted.

'No,' she denied stonily.

'Katie——'

'Don't call me that!' she snapped. 'And I don't
know why you keep bothering to justify yourself! You
don't like me! It can't possibly matter to you one way
or the other what I think of you!'

'Can't it?'

'No.'

With one finger beneath her chin, causing a long
shiver to go through her, he looked down into her
eyes. 'Can't it?' he repeated. 'It was you I wanted,
Kate, not Candida, not the memory of her, you.'

'Oh, wanting,' she managed airily, as though it
couldn't possibly matter to her one way or the other.

'Yes, Kate, wanting.'

'Well, don't. I don't want you to want me!'

'You don't?'

'No. And stop playing silly games!'

'Are they so silly, Kate?' he asked softly, persuasively. 'To want you, hold you, make love to you——'

'Don't,' she groaned.

'Why?'

'Because you don't like me! And you needn't think I'm fooled by this—this...'

'Seduction?' he breathed softly, his breath shivering across her mouth.

'Yes! Because I know what you're up to. You're trying to make me change my mind about the race!'

'Am I? So sure, Kate?'

'Of course I'm sure! Why else would you be doing it?'

'Why? To make amends, perhaps? I have treated you badly...'

'You've always treated me badly,' she said baldly. 'What's so different about now?'

'Because now I realise how wrong I was about you. Because I am ashamed at the way I have treated you, and because you are agitated and I wish to say sorry——'

'And to say that you wanted me!' she retorted waspishly. Her breath labouring in her lungs, her palms damp, she wished she could find the strength to push him away, run.

'Mmm, that too,' he agreed softly.

'Well, I don't want you to want me!' she told him, not sounding nearly so firm as she would have liked. 'And even if it was true, which I strongly doubt, it's hardly fair to Eleanor, is it?'

'Eleanor? Why should I need to be fair to Eleanor?'

'Oh, well, pardon me,' she muttered sarcastically. 'Obviously in Portugal it isn't necessary, or even considered gallant to be faithful to one's fiancée.'

'Fiancée? There is no contract between us.'

'Carlos said you were going to be married.'

'Did he?' he asked pensively. 'How extraordinary.'

'And you said she was to be your wife!'

'No, Kate, you said she was to be my wife.'

'Well, you said she was to share your table, your bed!'

'Mmm. You made me angry. I sometimes say things I shouldn't when I'm angry. But, I promise you, Eleanor is not to be my wife. You think I would choose wrongly again, after Candida? No, Kate, although she would be suitable——'

'Suitable!' she bit out in disgust. 'You make her sound like a prize heifer!'

With a soft little laugh, he trailed his finger across her mouth before moving both hands to the wall, one either side of her, his dark eyes humorous as he looked down into her stormy face. 'You are like a little fish struggling on the end of a line—and we both know that anglers are stronger than fish...'

'Not if they're sharks, they're not!' Grimly determined not to allow the pervasive quality of his voice to undermine her, she stared defiantly into his eyes. 'You might just as well give up, Adriao. I won't be persuaded.'

'You don't listen, Kate,' he reproved softly. 'I've already told you that isn't what I was trying to do. I was trying to restore the truce. I behaved badly towards you, a guest in my house—why the sudden sad look, Kate?'

Determinedly banishing the feeling, she glared at him. She was very likely to tell him why, wasn't she?

The fact that he only wanted a truce because she was a guest in his home, and presumably because he was frustrated!

'Truce?' he asked softly. Removing one hand from the wall, he held it out to her.

Staring at it, almost as though it might bite her, she flicked her eyes back to his and surprised a rather intent expression on his face before it became shuttered again. Truce? Well, why not? she thought defiantly. They were bound to meet again in the future. He and Peter were close friends, and if she remained within Peter's orbit they were bound to come across each other, and if she continued to be aggressive he would eventually wonder why, wouldn't he? And she didn't want him to know why. She didn't even want to admit it to herself.

'All right, truce,' she agreed.

'You have to shake hands, Kate,' he said softly.

No, she didn't, she thought, looking away from the persuasion in his eyes. If she touched him, she knew what would happen—and he would know how she felt.

'Kate?'

And if she didn't shake hands with him, he would also know how she felt. Taking a deep breath, she quickly thrust out her hand, and was unable to suppress her shudder as their palms touched. His clasp was firm, cool, decisive, like the man, and had she not had first-hand knowledge otherwise, she would have wondered if any warm blood flowed in those veins. Only she did have first-hand knowledge, and knew that his blood flowed hot, not warm. Anyone who controlled his emotions so rigidly had to be hiding something. Passion.

As she tried to tug her hand free, his clasp tightened, and she looked up, her heart stopping at the expression in his eyes.

'Yes,' he whispered. 'You, not Candida, nor Eleanor, you. Wanting, needing—like this...' Before she could jerk her head away, his mouth was warm against hers, a searing contact that robbed her of thought. 'And this,' he continued, 'and this,' his voice a low groan of need that found an echo inside her. As his body touched, ground against her, forcing her flat against the wall like a butterfly pinned to a board, she gave a long deep shiver and arched against him and their need spiralled out of control. It was like being swept up in a whirlwind, a vortex. There was no space anywhere between them as they kissed each other with a hunger too long denied. A fierceness, a violent exchange that robbed them of breath, of energy.

'A brute, hmm?' he asked thickly as his mouth moved to her chin, her neck and lingered there before moving to the lobe of her ear, and she shivered convulsively at the feelings he was generating.

'No,' she denied jerkily.

'And do I frighten you half to death, Kate?' he whispered huskily as he retraced the trail he had already burned into her flesh.

'No.'

'Perhaps it was never Candida,' he continued, his voice muffled, thick, as he reached the corner of her mouth. 'Perhaps always it was this, knowing the moment we met that you awoke this need, this wanting inside of me, and my reaction, the denials of a civilised man.'

'No...'

'No? No what?' he asked humorously as he fought for some sort of control.

'I don't know,' she murmured helplessly.

'No, neither do I.' Easing his weight away from her, he just as suddenly returned it and gathered her close, his mouth once more finding hers as though he could not possibly be denied its warmth for one moment longer. Yet now it was no longer urgent, but softer, more persuasive, frustratingly so, because she found she needed the demand, not the caution. Her arms wrapped round his neck, she forced him closer, increased the pressure of her mouth, until the harsh shrilling of the telephone made her jump and jerk away in shock. Opening dazed eyes, she stared at him almost blankly.

'Ignore it,' he breathed thickly as his mouth once more grazed across hers. Only the telephone had no intention of being ignored. It sounded shriller, if anything, demanding answer.

With a muttered oath, he dragged himself away, walked across the room and snatched up the phone. *'Sim?'* he barked.

Her body shaking, she leaned limply back against the wall and watched him. A warm flush lay along his high cheekbones, and his body was still tense—aching? As was hers? She felt numb, exhausted, shocked at her own response, at not knowing herself at all. She had wanted to bite into his lip, score her fingers down his back—and have him do the same to her. Dear God, she thought on a shuddering breath, surely normal, ordinary people didn't want to behave like that? A brute, he'd said of himself. What then did that make her?

Staring at him, as he spoke impatiently into the phone, common sense reasserted itself, and she began to think instead of just react. Had she allowed herself to believe his soft words just because she wanted to? Because she wanted him? He'd said he wanted her—but only because he knew that was what she wanted? Because he had suddenly remembered her response in his bathroom? He was an experienced man, probably knew a lot of women, understood what made them tick. And he needed her to drive in the race.

On the other hand, he hadn't been entirely unmoved. He had wanted her, but only because he was a normal male animal and any woman would have done? His movements, gestures were impatient—because he'd been interrupted so near to success? Or because he did truly want her? As she watched, he pulled a face of disgust and raked one hand through his hair before jabbering away in his own language. Giving orders? Demanding an explanation? She had no way of knowing. She didn't understand a word he said, but it would be a good opportunity to escape, give herself time to think. Rebuild the wall?

Still off balance, and, in truth, feeling rather shamed by her response, she walked quietly out and closed the door just as one of the manservants walked swiftly along the hall to open the front door.

Hovering uncertainly, she gave a lame smile at the man who entered. Small, portly, bald. He gave her a beaming smile and launched into a flood of Portuguese.

With a comical expression of dismay, she tried to break in, '*Desculpe,* excuse me, *não compreendo...*'

'Ah, excuse, *senhora,* my apologies. You are of course the English young lady who is to drive——'

'No,' she began just as Carlos erupted from the back room and launched into his own flood of Portuguese.

'I hope you are telling him he's made a mistake, Carlos,' she said warningly as she forcibly dragged her mind and emotions out of the study. Her eyes narrowing on his guilty face, she added firmly, 'I am not driving.'

'Not?' the newcomer asked in confusion. 'But Carlos, he say——'

'I can just imagine what Carlos say, but his little ruse didn't work.'

'Ruse?' Carlos asked innocently, his eyebrows practically climbing into his grey hair. 'What ruse is that, Kate?'

'You know very well what ruse! The one you and Adriao worked out before he came into the study...' And she knew suddenly that she was right. Knew by his innocent expression what she had known from the moment Adriao sought her out, yet had still allowed herself to be manipulated. Staring at him, she felt sick, and cheated, and a fool.

With a look of blank incomprehension that wouldn't have fooled a four-year-old, he denied quietly, 'But I know of no ruse. What is it that Adriao has done?'

'You know very well what he's done.'

'But no. Tell me...' he persuaded, his eyes full of laughter.

'I have no need to tell you!' she exploded, her voice choked. 'And if you think that a little——' Breaking off, her face flushing, she glared at him.

'A little...?' he prompted softly, then chuckled unrepentantly when she stormed off towards the terrace.

How could Carlos find it amusing? she thought in hurt bewilderment. How could she have let Adriao touch her? she demanded of herself. How could she allow a man she disliked to—to—mould her like putty? Always wanted you! Well, perhaps he had, and then used her own response as a lever to get his own way. What a real gullible little ninny he must think her! A few soft words, a—devastating kiss? her mind insinuated. And she wanted him. Dear God, she thought, appalled. How could she want him? How could she not have known that her continual fighting with him was because—because what? Because she wanted him to like her and he didn't? Feeling mortified that he should know and immediately understand, and she hadn't, she stared blindly out across the garden, and one hand stole unconsciously up to touch her mouth. As soon as she became aware of what she was doing, she snatched her hand away.

Had he known how inexperienced she was? That it would be easy to confuse her? Yes, he had, she remembered, because on the drive here he'd asked if she was afraid of men. Yes, she'd said, not afraid precisely, wary... And he'd played on that, because he needed her to drive in the race. And you're in love with him. Staring blindly before her, she finally admitted the stark truth. She was in love with him— and how the gods must be falling about in hysterics. Plain, aggressive, wealthy Kate Lassiter who had so consistently held men at bay because she doubted anyone could possibly want her for herself, only her money, had finally fallen in love with a man who only wanted her to drive in a race.

Throwing herself into one of the chairs dotting the terrace, she held herself rigid as she tried to shut out the moments in his arms. And if the telephone hadn't interrupted them? Then she jumped and looked away as Adriao came to stand in front of her. Stared down into her face.

Leaning forward, he put a hand on each arm of her chair, trapping her. 'No,' he said softly. 'Look at me.' When she did so, her eyes defiant, trying to hide the pain, he whispered again, 'No.'

'No what?'

'No, it was not a deliberate plan to make you agree. No, it was not false. I kissed you, held you, because I wanted to. Because I have——' then broke off with a curse as they heard footsteps coming out to the terrace. Straightening, he turned away and went to stand a few feet from her and stare out over the garden, as she had.

'Come on, Kate,' Carlos said cajolingly as he padded out behind her, 'you know you want to. Think of the excitement, the challenge—and you wouldn't really want to see us scratch, would you? Think of Peter.'

'I don't want to think of Peter,' she denied, her mind more on Adriao's words than Carlos's pleas.

'But he would be so happy. And think what a nice ending it will make to the article. Please?' he begged, coming round to stand in front of her, ignoring Adriao. 'We would be so grateful...'

'That's emotional blackmail, Carlos.'

'True,' he agreed outrageously, 'but I don't know what else to try. Would it be so impossible, Kate? A few days out of your life to help us? You'd get a cup...'

'If we won.'

'But of course we will win!' he exclaimed as though the matter were in no doubt at all.

'Oh, Carlos,' she said tiredly. 'It's not that I don't want to do it, you know it's not.'

'No, but if Adriao promises to be on his best behaviour...'

With a rude snort, she began picking at a flake of wood on the arm of the chair until Carlos grabbed her hand and stilled the movement.

'Oh, Kate, I could not bear it if Mandel's team wins. We'd never hear the last of it. Please? Eduardo has the papers here. All you have to do is sign...'

'And what am I supposed to do about my car?'

'We could have it driven over for you,' he said eagerly, as he sensed a weakening, 'or you could come back for it, whatever arrangements you want to make, and Peter would be so——'

'Will you please stop hurling Peter into the conversation?' she exploded, and when he gave such a comical expression of contrition her lip quivered, and she sighed. 'Is it so very important?' she asked fatalistically.

'Yes, Kate. With the publicity the race will generate, the Ferreira name will become better known, Adriao will make more profits to channel into his building programme, his tourism...'

'Oh, all right,' she agreed defeatedly, 'I'll——'

With a yell of delight, he shouted for Eduardo, and the portly little man came bustling out, a beam of pleasure on his round face, race papers clutched in one fist, pen in the other.

'The *senhora* will sign?'

'Not without reading them, she won't,' she said firmly. Taking the papers from him and giving Carlos a look of disgust, her eyes determinedly avoiding Adriao's still figure, she looked down, then up, an expression of defeat on her face. 'They're in Portuguese.'

'I'll translate them for you,' Carlos said eagerly.

'You will not, Eduardo will translate them for me. I don't trust you.'

'Nor me, Kate?' Adriao asked softly, coming to stand beside her once more.

Stiffening, feeling heat suffuse her cheeks, she kept her face resolutely averted. 'I don't know,' she muttered. 'Eduardo? And the pair of you can keep quiet; I don't want any whispered instructions to Eduardo to alter the content.' Handing the papers back to the other man, she folded her arms across her chest, and waited.

'Well, they seem quite straightforward,' she admitted grudgingly when Eduardo had finished reading. 'Although there didn't seem to be any mention of only one substitution, did there?' she asked Carlos.

'Er—no, I must have misread them.'

'Yes,' she agreed drily. 'So you must.'

'So you will sign?'

With a big sigh, she took the pen and quickly scribbled her name along the bottom before she could change her mind. Carlos seemed to be of the same opinion, because he whipped the papers away so quickly that it was laughable.

'So what happens now?' she asked, her mouth twisted into a wry grimace.

'Nothing happens now, except we peruse all maps assiduously,' Adriao said softly. He sounded as though he was smiling, damn him. Turning to glare at him, she found his dark eyes full of warmth, and a gleam of something else that she wasn't quite so sure of. Hastily looking away, she hurriedly scrambled to her feet as Carlos escorted Eduardo out. No way was she going to be left alone with Adriao.

'Kate?' he called softly, and she stiffened and came to a halt, her back to him. 'I did not lie to you——'

'I don't want to talk about it,' she broke in quickly. 'I've said I'll drive, and I will.'

'You can't run from me forever, Katie. When the race is over, when we can be alone, then we will talk—and you will admit what we both already know. Kate?'

Turning slowly to face him, she stared at him, her expression lost and uncertain, no trace of aggression or defiance.

'All right?' he asked again. Gently, as though he was concerned.

'All right,' she agreed with a jerky little nod.

'Good. Don't look so tragic, it will be all right, I promise.'

Would it? she wondered later as she lay in bed, her hands clasped behind her head. What would be all right? He's taken my armour away, she thought, feeling frightened and vulnerable, and I don't know if I'll be able to put it back. They'd become lovers? Is that what he meant? And when they'd finished being lovers? What then? All he'd said was that he wanted her, wanted to hold her, kiss her. Despite what he thought she was? She didn't think she wanted to be taken on those terms—but she did want to be wanted. As he very well knew.

Throughout the last, difficult week, she kept her feelings on a very tight rein, not allowing herself to speculate. She was polite, helpful, reserved, and she felt as though she was coming apart. Most of her remarks were addressed to Carlos as he tested herself and Adriao on the names of towns, villages, major roads, landmarks that were en route to all the European capitals. They could be going to Berne, Vienna, Rome, Amsterdam, Brussels, Paris, or London. No one would know until a few minutes before the race was to start so they needed a good working knowledge of the names of towns to make for leading to each capital. Each Portuguese driver was to be accompanied by a driver from one of the countries taking part and each would be handed an envelope naming their destination, currency for the countries to be driven through and a list of the checkpoints they must visit.

'Remember the car will be searched before the start. No maps, diaries that might contain maps, compass, or any other aid to travel is to be taken,' Carlos reiterated. 'Passports, currency of your choice, credit cards, personal clothing are all you are allowed. Don't try to sneak anything in. If anything contrary to the rules is found, you will be penalised.'

'What about food? Flasks of coffee? Cold drinks?' she asked, still determinedly avoiding discussing anything directly with Adriao whose face often wore that expression of hateful amusement.

'A container of water is only allowed, either for car or human. Food you must get en route so that all are equal and must stop for refreshment. No extra petrol must be taken, but you will be allowed an emergency kit, fan belt, spare bulbs et cetera. So, you will please both make a list of all the things you wish to take, then we will again go over the best route across Spain to the French border.'

And so it went on. The trips out in the race car to familiarise themselves with it. Adriao regarding her with lazy amusement, Kate being determinedly efficient, and neither referring directly to the incident that had taken place in the study, or his enigmatic words afterwards. Not that she'd forgotten them; she couldn't, and she still wasn't sure whether she could forgive him for making her aware of him in a way she hadn't been aware before. Because he'd been wrong about that, she finally decided, she hadn't known the first time she saw him. Had felt only dislike. And now? Now she just felt confused, and aching, and wouldn't allow herself to think about what would happen when the race was over. She still thought it was asking for trouble being in the same car with him for a long journey, but she was also beginning to feel a determination to do well. To win. And she had to admit that part of her, a major part of her, was looking forward to it. To the challenge, and, yes, the excitement. There would be no time for personal exchanges of any kind, their concentration would be all on the race, which was how it should be, and she could cope with that, couldn't she? So why did she keep yearning for him to touch her? To kiss her as he had in the study? Reassure her? He watched her, she knew he did, his eyes gentle, amused, but not once did he touch her. Why? Because now that he'd got his own way he didn't need to?

Then, suddenly, before she was sure she was ready, it was the morning of the race. She was woken at six by the little maid Maria and when she'd showered and dressed in loose-fitting cotton trousers and short-sleeved shirt she joined Adriao and Carlos for a sub-stantial breakfast.

'Don't drink too much,' Carlos warned as Kate poured herself another coffee, and when she looked puzzled, he chuckled. 'Adriao won't be very pleased if you have to stop every five minutes to find a ladies' room.'

'Oh,' she exclaimed softly, then gave him a cha-grined grin. 'Sorry, I didn't think.'

'Nervous?' Adriao asked softly, an odd smile in the back of his eyes.

Giving him a look of surprise that he should understand, she nodded, confessing, 'It's ridiculous, I know, but my tummy is full of butterflies. I know I didn't want to do this, but now that I am...'

'You don't want to let us down,' Adriao finished for her, and again, surprisingly, gave what could only be called a satisfied nod. 'Ready?'

With a wry smile, she got to her feet. 'As I'll ever be, I guess. Coming to see us off?' she asked Carlos.

'Of course. I shall be staying at the race headquarters to monitor your progress. The check-points will ring in as and when each vehicle passes.'

The race was scheduled to start at seven-thirty outside the wine caves in the Avenue Diogo Leite, but first they had to go to the race headquarters for the final briefing, to receive the result of the draw and to see who would be driving the first leg of the race. As Adriao gave his own car into the hands of the mechanic, who in turn gave him the keys to the race car with a wide grin and a slap on the back that made Adriao stagger, she and Carlos began to transfer their belongings, butterflies still struggling for supremacy in her stomach.

As soon as Adriao had reassured himself that the car was as he had last seen it, he allowed Kate to take the driving seat and drive them the short distance to the office for one last practice. When she'd parked in the space indicated, they all went inside to be greeted by the noisy enthusiasm of the other drivers and officials who all seemed to be talking at once.

'Hey, Adriao! Where is Peter?' Marcel exclaimed as he rushed across, and, much to Kate's embarrassment, gave her an exuberant hug.

'Ill, and kindly keep your hands to yourself,' he said smoothly as he physically removed Marcel's arms from around her and returned them to his sides.

'Ill? Since from when?' he asked in astonishment. 'He was all right——'

'Carlos,' Adriao interrupted, 'take Kate away and find her a seat, will you?' With a brief smile, he gave Kate a little push towards his uncle. 'I'll join you in a minute.'

Towed unceremoniously away, she stared back at the two men in astonishment, saw Adriao say something and the Frenchman laugh before they were lost from sight as the other drivers came between them. And, what was even more extraordinary, every time someone came up to greet her, Carlos became spokesperson and wouldn't allow her to get a word in edgeways.

'What is this? A conspiracy?' she demanded as Adriao finally joined them.

'Conspiracy, Kate?' he asked blandly. 'Now why should you think that?'

'Because every time someone comes up to talk to me, either you or Carlos hustles me away!'

'Nonsense. Now pay attention, Kate, Eduardo is about to speak.'

Giving him a fulminating glance, she pursed her mouth and turned her attention to Eduardo, then gave a snort of exasperation. 'I'd like to know how I'm supposed to pay attention,' she whispered irritatedly, 'when I can't understand above one word in twenty.'

'I'll translate,' he promised smoothly.

Which he did, quite obviously taking her literally and translating every blessed word.

'At each designated check-point, we change over and the other drives; if the check-points are more than

four hours apart, then the four-hour mark is the signal
to change and the time is to be noted on the race card.
At each check-point we hand the card in to be
stamped; anyone arriving at the ultimate destination
who doesn't have sufficient number of stamps is dis-
qualified. The first to reach the destination, providing
no penalty points have been incurred, is the winner.
If two or more cars have an equal time, it is the one
with the least penalties who wins. There will be
helicopter support and a fluorescent disc, which will
be provided, is to be placed on the roof of the car if
we are in need of mechanical or accident assistance.
And he wishes us good luck,' he concluded with a
warm grin, looking as unlike the Adriao she thought
she was coming to know as possible. He looked suddenly boyish, filled with enthusiasm and humour, and,
forgetting her irritation, she grinned back.

Giving her shoulder a little pat, he went forward to
collect his envelope with the destination and currency
and to be told the name of the first driver. Watching
him, the camaraderie he shared with the other drivers,
the easy way he chatted to them, sharing a joke
perhaps, the lithe grace with which he walked, the
long legs encased in loose cotton trousers for comfort
on the long drive, the dark hair ruffled attractively
across his forehead, she was suddenly glad she had
agreed. Maybe she did love him to no end, but
perhaps, just perhaps, it would be all right, as he had
said, and the small niggle of excitement that she had
been so busily suppressing flared into unexpected life.
Hoping against hope that she wasn't being a fool, that
she wasn't deceiving herself, she allowed herself a
small foolish dream that he might come to love her
in return.

Aware of someone coming to stand beside her, she turned her head, and smiled at the Frenchman.

'Hello, again. All set?'

'*Oui. Bonne chance*, Kate,' he murmured, a wicked twinkle in his dark eyes as he kissed her on each cheek.

'And you.' Still smiling faintly, she jumped as Adriao materialised beside her.

'*Bonne chance*, Marcel, and *au'voir*,' he added firmly and clearly with every intention of being obeyed.

With a little chuckle, Marcel drifted away to join his co-driver.

'Anyone would think you didn't want me to speak with him!' she declared as Adriao began manoeuvering her towards the doors. 'That's the second time you've done that!'

'And there will be a third, fourth and fifth time, my Kate, if you persist in disobeying me.'

'But why? He was only being friendly! Anyone would think you were jealous!' When he didn't answer, she turned her head to look at him. 'Well?'

His eyes suddenly dancing with laughter, he kissed the corner of her mouth. 'Of course I am jealous. Now come.'

If he was jealous, which she strongly doubted, why had he been so amused? 'I haven't said goodbye to Carlos . . .'

'Carlos will understand,' he said arrogantly. 'And you're driving first leg.'

'What?'

'I said——'

'I heard what you said!' she retorted, irritated all over again.

Grinning at her, totally unrepentant, he gave her a hug that she wasn't sure she found in the least comforting. Yet the warmth of him, the strength, was something to be savoured, and in the bustle to get out to the cars she dismissed his odd behaviour over Marcel as nothing more than last-minute nerves. The fact that Adriao never seemed to have any nerves she conveniently ignored, because she didn't think his behaviour could have been generated by jealousy. And if it wasn't jealousy, it had to be nerves, didn't it?

When they returned to the car, Kate saw that the advertising boards had been fixed, mounted on a roof-rack. FERREIRA PORT in big bold letters, burgundy on cream. There was also a green sticker on the door to prove it had been searched. Their hand luggage had also been searched. Their persons were searched before they were allowed to get into the car, and then, and only then, were they allowed to open the envelope.

Holding her eyes for a moment, spinning out the tension, he took a deep breath and ripped it open. 'Hotel Metropole, Paris,' he pronounced softly.

'That will favour Marcel and Vitor, won't it? Unless you are familiar with the city?'

'Not very, no,' he denied. 'I have been there, of course . . .'

'Oh, of course,' she teased.

His eyes full of laughter, he dropped a light kiss on her nose, then, taking her by surprise, tugged her forward and kissed her very thoroughly on the mouth. Before she could restore her equilibrium, he continued smoothly, 'Now, make sure you are comfortable, that the seat is in the right position, put your seatbelt on, and then relax. We have five minutes.'

'Yes,' she agreed blindly as she continued to stare at him in confusion. Then, taking a deep, calming breath, she wriggled herself into position, snapped her seatbelt in place, and slowly followed the car in front

down to the start. Tugging on the handbrake, leaving
the engine running, she stared resolutely through the
windscreen and forced herself to relax.

Sunlight winked and sparkled on the supports of
the Ponte Dom Luis bridge that spanned the river on
their left. The port boats bobbed gently on the swell,
a soft breeze intermittently ruffling the distinctive
cream sails with the names of the wine caves to which
they belonged printed boldly across their fronts.
Glancing across the river to the Ribeiro, the old
quarter on the opposite bank, at the houses perched
precariously one above the other, she settled the
picture in her mind for her article; and to help still
the butterflies, and banish the warmth of Adriao's
kiss that still made her mouth tingle.

The sky was a clear, bright blue; crowds lined the
route and every so often she would see a flash as yet
another photograph was taken. Reporters? she wondered. Yet the thought was an absent one as she stared
at faces, committing them to memory, to take her
mind off herself and the knowledge that in a few
minutes she would be expected to make a smooth,
fast start. Her palms damp, she surreptitiously wiped
them on her thighs, then jumped in alarm as the crowd
let out a roar as the car in front of them set off. They
were next. Three minutes to go and her hands
tightened nervously on the wheel.

'Calm down,' Adriao soothed. He sounded calm,
relaxed, confident, and she gave him a resentful
glance. How could he sound so calm? 'Two minutes,
Kate,' he continued, his eyes now on his watch.

'Right,' she whispered huskily, her eyes fixed ahead
until they ached.

'One. Remember, don't snatch at the clutch, a nice
smooth getaway. You'll be fine.'

'I feel sick,' she muttered. 'Oh, Adriao, I don't think I can do it,' she wailed, sudden panic making her voice wobble. 'I'll stall the engine; hit the kerb; get penalty points...' and, unbelievably, he laughed. A rich warm chuckle that made her swing towards him in astonishment.

'You'll be fine,' he comforted. 'Take a deep breath, relax.' Then, before she could do so, he began to count the seconds off for her. 'Five, four, three, two—go.'

Thankfully, he didn't shout it, which would have panicked her, just said it smoothly, calmly, and without her consciously being aware of it her right foot went down, the left up, and they got smoothly away. Into second, third, change down for the turning on to the bridge, and she gave a nervous laugh of relief. They were away.

# CHAPTER SIX

VILA REAL, Braganca, San Martin and the change-over at the border; Zamora, Valladolid, Palencia, through villages, towns, flat open stretches as they raced the sun towards the two-hour stop-over point in Santander. At first, adrenalin and excitement made the miles slip by, but, gradually, as they neared the next check-point, tiredness began to cramp their muscles, dull their minds, and the last few hours were completed in silence.

Whether they were just lucky, or whether everyone had made very sure to keep farm trucks off the road so as not to block their route, Kate didn't know, but they reached the dual carriageway leading to the ancient Spanish town in just under twelve hours with Kate driving the final leg.

'Time?' she asked quietly.

'Almost seven-thirty.'

'That's pretty good, isn't it? A lot faster than the drive out.'

'*Sim*, Kate,' Adriao agreed softly, 'and a lot more—comfortable.'

Slanting him a look of amusement, she followed the signs for the ferry terminal where they were to check in. 'Almost there,' she murmured thankfully.

'Mmm. Tired, Kate?'

'A bit achy—I shan't be sorry to stretch my legs.'

'No, nor I.'

As she pulled in through the port gate, she just had time to notice that there was another race car already parked before they were engulfed in an army of reporters and photographers all shouting at once.

'*Deus,*' Adriao exclaimed softly as Kate accelerated away and into the space provided for them. Hastily shoving his card at the race official to be stamped, he added quickly, 'I'll deal with them, you go and claim our rooms at the Hotel Bahia, and organise a meal. Over there, see?' he explained pointing across the busy junction to the big hotel on the corner.

Grabbing her bag, she climbed out and had taken no more than two steps when she turned curiously back as she heard someone calling Adriao. An excited feminine voice, and, as she watched, a tall, young, and very beautiful woman dressed in tailored cream skirt and silk shirt came out of the building ahead of them and hurried over, her arms held wide. Well, she certainly wasn't intending to greet herself, Kate thought; she'd never seen her before in her life. Turning to look at her companion, she saw that he was grinning. As the woman reached him, Adriao spread his arms and caught her up in a bear-hug, lifting her off her feet, and, in front of the laughing officials and cheering reporters, he kissed her. Long and hard—and extremely passionately. Feeling a sharp stab of jealousy, she turned quickly away. Did he have women at every check-point ready to congratulate him? she wondered. Wish him well? He'd never greeted her with such enthusiasm.

Feeling the old dreadful insecurity rushing back, she dashed blindly across the road, dangerously dodging the traffic amid hoots and hurled abuse, all of which she ignored, and pushed into the hotel. Feeling hot, dirty—and hurting, because if he could kiss the dark-haired beauty with such warmth and passion, he couldn't feel a hell of a lot for her, could he? Which meant he had only been nice to her because he wanted her to drive in the race and for no other reason. Which she had always suspected, but, childishly, hadn't wanted confirmed.

Waiting quietly in the short queue at the reception desk she tried desperately to shut out the picture in her mind. Don't over-react, she kept telling herself, it probably doesn't mean anything. Don't let suspicion colour your judgement. When the smiling receptionist reached her, she showed the Port Race badge she'd been given, and collected her key. Avoiding the many curious stares she was receiving, she made her way to the lifts just as Adriao hurried in, the dark-haired woman still on his arm.

'All right?' he asked with a smile. 'You have organised the rooms?'

'A room,' she said shortly, holding up the key.

'And a meal?'

'No,' she muttered, avoiding his eyes as she turned away to stab at the lift button, 'I don't speak Spanish.'

'And they don't speak English?' he asked quietly, his eyes narrowed slightly.

'No.' In no mood to explain that she hadn't even asked about a meal, she muttered, 'It's room 813.' As the lift came to a thumping halt before her, she pulled open the old-fashioned door then dragged the metal grille aside and stepped inside. Whipping the door shut and replacing the grille, she stabbed the button for the eighth floor, and, for once in her life, something went right. With a groan of machinery, the lift began to ascend before Adriao could follow her. Bastard, she thought. They were all the same.

It seemed to take forever for the lift to grind and shudder its way up, and when it finally lurched to a stop she scrabbled her way out feeling claustrophobic and shaky. She'd behaved abominably, and jealousy was absolutely no excuse whatsoever. She might try to justify it with being tired, tense, but it wouldn't be true. She'd watched Adriao and the dark woman kiss and had felt as though the world had come to an end. How stupid could you get?

Walking hesitantly down the corridor, staring at door numbers, she wandered all the way down one long hallway before discovering she had to retrace her steps because the numbering, for some reason, wasn't consecutive. Feeling stupid and gauche, she walked back past the head of the stairs just as Adriao came bounding athletically up them. As he saw her, he came to a halt, his face as set as hers.

'Don't ever,' he said quietly, 'slam a door in my face again.' Taking the key from her, he walked without any of the confusion she'd experienced to the end of the hallway and inserted the key in the lock of the door facing them. Holding it wide, he waited for her to enter first.

Staring at him, at his arrogant face, his self-righteous pose, she fought to hold on to her control. Stalking towards him, head held high, she swept past him into the suite and through the nearest door into the bedroom. A door open on the far side showed the bathroom, and flinging her bag on to one of the single beds she went to stand at the window, her vision blurred by tears.

'Katherine,' he began quietly.

'Don't talk to me,' she muttered resentfully, and she heard him give a long sigh.

'Very well,' he agreed in a quiet, hateful voice, 'I suggest you go and have your shower. We don't have time to waste. I'll try and get through to Carlos, update him on our progress.'

Without answering, she snatched her bag off the bed and went into the bathroom. She hadn't been the one wasting time!

Fool, she castigated herself as she stood beneath the cooling spray. Why not emblazon it in forty-foot-high letters that you're jealous? Why not just stamp it on your forehead? Scrubbing shampoo into her hair until her head hurt, thoroughly irritated and cross with herself, she rinsed it and turned off the shower. Rubbing her hair almost dry and dressing in clean underwear, trousers and shirt, she slapped moisturiser on her face and glared at herself in the mirror, hating herself and her inability to come to terms with her new-found feelings for Adriao. Hating him for not being what she wanted. It was all right for men, she thought miserably, they didn't have to go through all this. They could fancy someone, and tell them, and it was all right!

Running a brush through her short hair, she crammed everything into her bag and returned to the bedroom. Adriao was lying back on the bed, completely at ease, his hands beneath his head, and as she came through he uncoiled himself, got lithely to his feet, picked up his own bag and went through into the bathroom. Staring after him, her eyes bleak, she swung away and threw herself on to one of the beds. If he thought she was going to be the one to apologise, he could think again! *She* hadn't done anything wrong. Picking up the telephone instruction leaflet, she quickly scanned it. She'd ring Jackie. Explain about the race, find out how Chris was.

When Adriao came out, dressed in clean heavy cotton beige trousers and a dark cream shirt, freshly shaved, his hair still damp from his shower, she was just replacing the receiver, and at his look of haughty enquiry explained defiantly, 'I was just calling Christopher.'

'How is he?'

'Fine.'

'Good. Ready? I ordered a meal.'

'Fine.'

Getting up, she picked up her bag only to drop it from nerveless fingers as he caught hold of her and swung her to face him. Linking his hands behind her waist, he looked down into her troubled eyes.

'Katherine, Katherine,' he said gently, 'don't you ever stop strewing your path with boulders? Don't you trust anyone?'

'I don't know,' she mumbled. 'So who was she?'

'Mandel's wife, Roseanne.'

'Then why...?'

'Why was she kissing me?' he teased, deliberately misunderstanding. 'Because she was pleased to see me, I expect. We're very good friends. She kisses her husband, too,' he added blandly. 'Now come along and stop being silly.' Dropping a light kiss on her nose, he retrieved her bag and ushered her out.

Silly? Confused, and not at all sure she felt comforted, she walked quietly beside him and down the stairs. 'Did you find out whom the other car belonged to?'

'*Sim*. It was Vitor.'

'How far ahead of us is he?'

'Ten minutes only,' he told her absently as he steered her across the lobby and into the restaurant where a table was already laid for them. Courteously seating her, he took the chair opposite, indicated she should begin eating and then applied himself to his own food.

Staring down at her plate, she jabbed her fork into the salad, not sure she was very hungry. How old was an old friend? she wondered. Had she gone out with Adriao before she married Mandel?

'Katherine,' Adriao said softly, his forearms resting on the table as he stared across at her, 'eat.'

Briefly raising troubled eyes to his, she gave a wan smile.

'Did you once go out with her?' she blurted.

'No, and if you don't stop picking away at the subject the way you're picking at that meal, I shall begin to think you're jealous.'

With a scornful little laugh that didn't quite come off, she denied aloofly, 'Why should I be jealous? I was just curious, that's all.'

'Of course,' he agreed smoothly, only she had the horrible feeling he was laughing at her.

Glad of a distraction, she looked round as she heard a commotion outside the restaurant, and saw Vitor and Marcel erupt in, both laughing.

Spotting them, they came over. Slapping Adriao on the back and grinning at Kate, Vitor and his co-driver grabbed a chair each and sat down.

'We'll join you,' he declared without waiting to be invited. Snapping his fingers at a passing waiter, he ordered more plates and cups.

'Thank you, Vitor,' Adriao said smoothly, a hint of amusement in the back of his dark eyes as he halted the waiter before he could carry out Vitor's order. 'It is no doubt an offer we should be unable to refuse; however, I'm sure you will be more comfortable over there.' Pointing to a table that was as far from them as it was possible to get, he spoke quickly to the waiter, who nodded enthusiastically and practically fell over himself in his eagerness to be of service. Turning back to his fellow countryman, he gave a smile that Kate was very glad wasn't turned on her. 'Don't keep the waiter waiting, Vitor. We will no doubt see you in Paris.'

'Just because you organised the race, my friend,' Marcel put in, 'and it is of the utmost importance to you——'

'Goodbye, Marcel, Vitor,' he added with an autocratic little dip of his head. 'I believe your table is now ready.'

With a grunt of laughter, Vitor got reluctantly to his feet. 'Come, Marcel,' he said, his tone heavy with resignation, 'the Baron has spoken.'

With a broad wink for Kate, Marcel got to his feet and followed Vitor to the other side of the restaurant.

'Close your mouth, Kate, you look exceedingly foolish with it hanging open like that,' Adriao commented without change of tone or expression. Picking up the coffee-pot, he refilled their cups. 'Eat,' he commanded softly.

Absently doing as he said, she asked quietly, 'Why didn't you want them to join us?'

'Because I wanted you to myself.'

Staring at him, her face comically registering her incredulity, she went pink when he gave her a slow smile that wasn't entirely comforting. Hastily looking down, she began to eat. 'Why did he call you the Baron?'

'It is what all my friends call me. It is a joke.'

'Because they think you're feudal?'

With a look of utter blandness, he shook his head. 'No, because my grandfather was. I look very much like him.'

She bet it wasn't because of his grandfather, or, only partly, maybe. Didn't he know how he appeared to others? 'You didn't speak to Vitor as though he was your friend,' she contradicted, giving him a quick look.

'Did I not?' Glancing across at Vitor, who caught his glance and grinned, he said softly, 'But he is a friend, Kate—although his understanding is not superior. Now,' he continued, as he checked his watch, 'it's just after eight-fifteen, so we——'

'Dear God,' she exclaimed quietly. 'You are so arrogant.'

'Of course,' he agreed as though it were the most natural thing in the world. 'As I was saying, we have another half-hour before our allotted two hours is up, which means we will have very little daylight left. A pity; I was hoping not to have to negotiate the Cantabrian mountains in the dark——'

'I expect you'll manage,' she couldn't resist pointing out.

Staring at her, his eyes suddenly filled with laughter. 'Back to normal now?'

With a faint smile, she pushed her plate away and picked up her coffee.

'With luck we will reach the French border before the end of my leg, which leaves possibly another eight hours to get to Paris. Not exactly a problem.'

'It might be for me,' she confessed quietly. 'I don't see very well in the dark.'

'Admitting to faults, Kate?' he teased gently.

'I've never not admitted to faults,' she told him with a superior little look of her own. 'I know I have a great many. Are we ready now?'

'Yes, Kate,' he agreed, his voice still laced with amusement. 'We're ready.'

Gulping down the last of her coffee, she got to her feet. 'I'd better just go to the loo. I'll meet you in Reception. Have you got the room key?'

'Yes, Kate, I have the key, but there's no rush, you know, we have plenty of time. If we leave before the allotted two hours, we incur penalty points.'

'And we mustn't do that, must we?'

It wasn't fair, she thought, to have so much charm, to be able to bend people to your will so easily. She'd been hurt and angry, determined to have it out with him, and she'd got up from the table as confused as when she'd sat down.

When she came out of the ladies', she saw Adriao, Vitor and Marcel chatting together, and she walked slowly across.

'We must go. *Até logo*, Kate,' Vitor said with a warm smile. 'We will see you in Paris. Hopefully, after we have arrived.' Punching Adriao lightly on the shoulder, he began walking away. 'Come, Marcel.'

'*Bonne chance*, Kate.' With a wicked look at Adriao from the corner of his eye, Marcel leaned forward and kissed Kate full on the mouth, and, because she was still feeling a little insecure, because Adriao hadn't really explained why he'd behaved as he had with Roseanne, she kissed him back.

'*Bonne chance*, Marcel,' she whispered as he hurried after Vitor.

'Even now, are we?' Adriao asked her, an expression that was very hard for her to read in his dark eyes.

'I didn't——'

'Didn't you? Come, we will return to the car.'

With a long sigh, she walked quietly beside him.

'And you will, in future, please stay away from Marcel,' he tacked on softly.

As they reached the pavement, they saw Mandel and his Italian co-driver, Roseanne between them, dodging the traffic and racing towards the hotel. As they ran past, Mandel grinned and shouted something and Adriao laughed, caught Kate's hand and hustled her equally dangerously between the traffic and back to the car.

'I thought he was your enemy?' she exclaimed breathlessly as she belted herself in.

'Who? Mandel? Good heavens, no! We've been friends for years!'

'Oh,' she said, nonplussed. 'Then why were you so determined to beat him in particular?'

'Because we're rivals, of course.'

Rivals for what? she wondered as the official indicated their two hours was up and they could now leave. The race prize? Or Roseanne?

They changed seats again at the French border, by which time Kate was beginning to feel slightly punch-drunk. Yawning widely and stretching her stiff muscles, she climbed behind the wheel.

'It's mostly motorway from here, Kate. You are all right? Not too tired?'

'No, I'm OK.'

'All right, let's go. We'll need to stop again for petrol, and perhaps get some coffee. If you begin to feel too tired, or cramped, let me know.'

And what? she wondered tiredly. You'll abandon the race? 'I'll be all right; I know how important it is to you.'

'Not more important than your safety, Kate. However, if you could manage to catch and pass Vitor...'

With a little smile, she settled down to the long drive ahead of them, and, as Adriao tilted his head back and closed his eyes, her mind reverted to the subject of Roseanne. Beautiful and elegant, someone from his own circle—everything she was not. As the miles

slipped past she found it harder and harder to con-
centrate. Achingly weary, her stomach feeling rather
peculiar because she had barely eaten anything all day,
her mind revolved uselessly over all that had happened since they'd arrived in Santander. But most of
all her mind retained the clear image of Adriao kissing
Roseanne. A vivid memory of his smile, his enthusiasm, his apparent passion.

Glancing briefly at her silent companion, she gave
a distressed little smile. Trust me, he'd said, but it was
so hard to believe he wanted her when there were
women like Roseanne around. Enclosed in a cocoon
of silence, she drove tiredly on. When Adriao stirred
and opened his eyes, she commented quietly, 'Not
much longer till we change over.'

'OK.' Hauling himself stiffly upright, he yawned.
'Lord, I think I'm getting too old for this.'

'Did you have a race last year?' she asked curiously.

'Mmm, not cars, power boats along the Douro.'

'Did you win?'

'Of course.'

Glancing at him, she saw him smile, his teeth
gleaming whitely in the darkness. 'And did Roseanne
kiss you then?' she asked, then could have bitten out
her tongue. Why in God's name couldn't she leave
the subject alone? she thought despairingly. 'Sorry,'
she muttered. 'I didn't mean to ask you that.'

'She is a friend, Kate,' he told her quietly, 'nothing
more, nothing less.'

'But once she was more?' she persisted, knowing
she should leave it alone, but quite unable to do so.

'No. Why do you find it so hard to believe me?'

'Because she's beautiful, I suppose—and you
looked as though you were enjoying it. It's a little
difficult to believe anything else when you go around

kissing and hugging any woman that comes along,'
she commented sadly.

'Any woman?' he asked quietly. 'How many women
have you seen me hugging and kissing, Kate?'

'Eleanor, Roseanne, me...' Her voice catching, she
took a deep breath before continuing, 'But just because I didn't see you with others doesn't mean there
weren't any.'

'So it doesn't. You have me pegged as some sort of
Don Juan?'

'No,' she denied stiffly. 'And Marcel said——'

'Ah, yes, Marcel,' he said with dangerous softness.

With an unhappy little sigh, she dragged her attention back to the road. To pursue it further would
send him back to that cold, aloof stranger she had so
disliked, and who she didn't ever want to see again.
Straightening in her seat, trying to ease the ache in
her back, she stared blindly through the windscreen,
unable to see anything but the illuminated road ahead,
cars rushing towards them on the other side of the
road.

'What time is it?' she asked quietly.

'Just after three-thirty.'

'Do we have time for a short break, do you think?'

'Of course, I myself could use a coffee and something to eat, and it is nearly time for us to change
over again.'

Easing her shoulders to dispel the stiffness, caused
partly by tension, she slowed her speed slightly, and,
as the lights of a service station came up, indicated
to pull in. Driving into the car park where one or two
lorries were parked in front of the restaurant, she
thankfully pulled on the handbrake and switched off
the engine. Stretching in the narrow confines of the
car, she groaned and yawned widely. When his warm

palm slid to her nape, she gave a little start of surprise and turned towards him.

His smile was gentle, his expression kind, and she felt a flood of emotion well up inside her, tightening her throat. Watching him, wanting him, hating the distance she herself had put between them, she put out a hesitant hand to touch his cheek, then gave a little shiver as he turned his mouth into her palm.

'It will be all right, Kate,' he reassured her softly. 'Trust me, hmm?'

'Yes, I'm sorry. It's just that . . .'

'I know.' Dropping another kiss in her palm, he slowly removed his hand from her neck. 'Not much longer now.'

'No. I shan't be sorry to get there.'

'Nor I. For many reasons. Come.'

Collecting her handbag, she climbed out and breathed deeply of the fresh night air. She could see lights twinkling in the distance: a small village perhaps, people rising early for work in the fields; could hear a dog barking, the comforting clatter of crockery from the restaurant, and it all seemed unreal. With a tired little sigh, she walked with him inside and they sat in one of the booths as a tired waitress came over to take their order.

Soup, crusty bread and butter, a honey cake each, for energy, Adriao said, and coffee.

Staring at him across the table, at his sleepy eyes, unshaven chin, and strong elegant hands as he cradled his coffee-cup, she felt her eyes prick with tears. I love you, she told him silently. Dear lord, how I love you.

As though aware of her scrutiny, he glanced up and his eyes crinkled with lazy humour. 'If you continue to look at me like that, Kate, we will not finish the race. Tell me about the centre you're hoping to set up,' he encouraged.

Flushing, she looked down, then pulled a funny little face. 'Oh, so you know about it, do you?'

'Yes. Peter and I had a long talk while you were away, about a lot of things. I treated you very badly, didn't I? I'm sorry. So tell me now while we eat. How did the idea start?'

'With a friend, Sally, who looked after her elderly mother, always fraught, afraid to leave her, afraid to go on holiday without taking her, and, when they did take her, it was no break because her mother was so difficult, senile. So I sometimes used to go and granny-sit, just to give them a break.'

'They didn't consider putting her in a home?'

'Well, I think they probably did when she was at her most difficult, but, as Sally said, when you re-member what a lovely person she had been, so kind, helping them out when they'd first got married, she would have felt so guilty. All she really wanted was for perhaps a few days a month free, a holiday with her husband and children knowing that Granny was being well looked after. There seemed to be a lot of people like that,' she continued reflectively, 'with elderly relatives to care for. I like old people,' she exclaimed suddenly as though someone might doubt it. 'They are so gloriously selfish, like children. They're the most important people in their worlds. They accept you as you are and only query what af-fects them. Sally and I often discussed it, about how awful it must be, to grow old and not be wanted by anyone. And I suppose that's when the idea was born. I had a lot of money. The family were always wealthy; even when my parents split up, mother had sufficient funds to keep us in luxury,' she muttered disparagingly as she remembered the sybaritic existence that had never brought happiness. 'When she died it was left to me. Then, when my father died, the rest of the estate came to me. Money, a big house, why not utilise it? I wasn't quite philanthropic enough to give it all away,' she confessed as though it were something of which she should be ashamed. When he didn't comment, she went on, 'It began with Sally's mother, and, like Topsy, the idea just growed. Why not start a centre where people could leave their grannies or grandads for short stays? A day, a week maybe to give families a break. From there it seemed a natural progression to take in handicapped children; their families too sometimes needed a break. I couldn't believe how many there were in my area alone. The local doctor was enthusiastic, and his wife, a nurse, said they'd be willing to be on hand should I need them. So I got my solicitor to find out all the legal necessities, deal with the local council, and now I'm just waiting to hear if I can go ahead.'

'And Jean Barham knew of your idea, and that's why she left you her estate?'

'Yes. The money from the sale of the house is to be used to help fund the centre.'

'And Christopher is one of the handicapped children?'

'Yes,' she admitted softly. 'Peter tell you that, too?'

'Mmm.'

'So why did you never say?'

'Because I wanted you to tell me,' he said simply. 'And there is no one else in your life, Kate?' When she shook her head, he commented with quiet satisfaction, 'Good.' Reaching for her hand, he lifted it and pressed his mouth all too briefly against her knuckles. 'Time to go. We should reach Paris before the end of my leg, so all you need to do is sit beside me and keep me company.'

Nodding, she got to her feet. 'I'll just go and have a quick wash. Two minutes. I'll see you back at the car.'

'All right—and Kate?' he called softly, yet when she turned back he slowly shook his head, a faint smile in his eyes. 'No, never mind, it will keep. Go on, go and have your wash.'

Walking slowly towards the ladies' room, her mind blurred with exhaustion, she wondered idly what he had been going to say. Thank you? Sorry?

Quickly using the facilities, she hurried back outside where Adriao was already waiting. Opening the door for her, he walked round and strapped himself into his own seat.

Putting a handful of chocolate bars and chewing-gum on the shelf, he added, 'I also bought a couple of cans of cold drink and some milk if you get thirsty. Ready? Why don't you try and have a sleep?'

Nodding, she leaned back, and she did try, but the hum of the engine, the noise of the wheels, the inter-mittent stab of oncoming headlights, made it im-possible. Giving up, she opened her eyes and stared almost hynotised through her window as the sky began to lighten from black to grey. Mist floated eerily in the fields to either side of the car making everything seem unreal, dreamlike, and she rolled her head to look at Adriao. He was beginning to look distinctly piratical, she thought with a smile, his hair untidy, his jaw beginning to stubble, and yet, oddly enough, it only seemed to add to his attraction. She wanted to put out her hand, caress that stubbled cheek, wanted him to hold her, kiss her—the way he'd kissed Mandel's wife? With a deep sigh, she allowed her weighted lids to drop again and hovered somewhere between that half-waking, half-sleeping state where dreams were more kind than reality. Where she was beautiful and witty and charming—and loved.

'Paris coming up,' she heard him say softly, and she quickly opened her eyes. The mist was beginning to lift, she saw as she straightened attentively, the scenery beginning to change as they drove through the quiet, empty suburbs. There were one or two delivery vans about, a road sweeper who leaned on his broom to watch them pass, pigeons that lifted in a lazy swirl as though they were all too familiar with such interruptions, and, after a short detour for roadworks that confused them, they finally pulled into the forecourt of the Hotel Metropole. A large tree hung over a pitted and cracked fountain and she stared at it dully, her eyes unfocused, lacking the energy to move.

Adriao was slumped in his seat beside her and she turned to look at him as a sleepy race official bustled out of the hotel and took their card.

'Are we first?' she asked him.

'*Sim, senhora...*' Then he grinned as another car screeched up behind them. 'But only just.'

Within seconds, the scene had changed. Other marshals hurried out, followed by a scruffy-looking reporter, who blinked, became suddenly alert and dashed back inside to return moments later accompanied by a photographer. Adriao miraculously revived, climbed out and grinned at the driver of the car behind them. Vitor, not Mandel, and she wondered at what point they'd passed them on the road. Vitor had been ten minutes ahead in Santander.

When a race official kindly opened the door for her, she had no real option except to climb out.

Staggering slightly, she watched Adriao clap Vitor on the back and shake hands with the Frenchman. What happened to his dislike? she wondered. No longer any need for it? When Marcel smiled at her, she smiled tiredly back and walked to join him.

'You started out after us in Porto, didn't you?' she asked as she rested her aching body against the wing of his car while Adriao and Vitor spoke with the reporter.

'*Oui,*' he smiled, 'by three minutes.'

'So, if you aren't three minutes after us arriving, that makes you the winner, doesn't it?'

'Yes, I'm very much afraid it does. Unless we got penalty points, that is.' Turning to Vitor, he asked him something in his own language, which Kate didn't need translating, and Vitor's mock affronted expression gave her the answer. No penalty points.

Summoning up another smile, she held out her hand to Vitor. 'Congratulations.'

'*Obrigada, senhora,*' Vitor said with a little dip of his head as he returned her handshake with enthusiasm and a wide smile.

'And you, Marcel. *Très bien.*'

'*Merci, et vous.*' With one of his very charming smiles, discarding his tiredness like an old sock, he carried her hand to his lips and kissed her fingers. Then, with a very attractive chuckle, he grasped her shoulders and kissed her as he had done in Santander. 'It is much better, no? To kiss a beautiful woman, especially one with so much courage and charm.'

'And especially when there's a photographer to capture it on film?' she asked a trifle cynically as she noticed the way he posed.

'But of course,' he agreed, not one whit offended by her tone. 'I am naturally desolated that we have

beat you, and by such a very little, but...' With a
very Gallic shrug, he smiled and stepped back.

Just as they were being ushered inside, there was a
screech of tyres and Mandel erupted through the
gateway, narrowly missing the fountain. Braking to a
noisy halt, he leaped from his car and flung his arms
around as many of them as he could reach. Bursting
into a flood of Portuguese that made everyone but
Kate and Marcel, who obviously didn't understand
either, laugh, they all muddled into the hotel together
and were ushered up to the suite set aside for the cel-
ebration. Judging by the confusion everyone seemed
to be in, they obviously hadn't been expected to arrive
quite so early.

Glasses of Bucks Fizz were hastily produced and
handed round, and Kate stared down into hers with
a little moue of distaste. She'd much rather have had
a cup of coffee, and wondered if she had the energy
to ask. The rest of the race officials, obviously hastily
summoned from their beds, came to have a word with
each of them, but, at barely six o'clock in the
morning, the gesture was somewhat wasted. Or it was
on her; no one else seemed to find it odd. Overcome
by exhaustion, barely able to stand upright, she just
wanted to leave, be by herself.

'You are very tired, Katie?' Umberto, Mandel's
Italian co-driver, asked with a sympathetic look as he
came to lean against the wall beside her.

'Mmm,' she agreed absently, her eyes on Adriao as
he talked and laughed with his friends. He seemed to
have forgotten all about her, and she felt stupidly
excluded and unwanted. Tiredness, she tried to tell
herself, and probably it was mostly that, but it was
also a feeling of inadequacy. She didn't seem to belong
in this noisy throng, and, once back with his friends,

it hadn't taken Adriao long to forget her existence, had it? She had done all he asked and more—didn't she even rate a thank-you? Did he blame her for losing the race? If she had driven just that little bit faster...

# CHAPTER SEVEN

KATE barely noticed Umberto leaving her side and going to join the others as they all chatted, exchanged notes, whatever, all except Marcel who, like her, was standing alone, his eyes unfocused. As she continued to stare at Adriao, he looked up, gave her a small smile and a raised eyebrow, and thereafter ignored her, so, with determined bravado, she walked across to Marcel and linked her arm through his.

Turning his head, he gave her a tired smile. 'Hello, Kate. Had enough?'

'Yes, I can hardly keep my eyes open. I can't imagine where they all get their energy from,' she added, her voice brittle as she nodded towards the other drivers who seemed to be having a high old time; especially Adriao, he looked like the king holding court. Taller than the others, more impressive, more arrogant, she mentally added, determined on her course of masochism.

As she and Marcel talked desultorily, her eyes remained fixed on Adriao until he caught her glance, and this time his dark eyes held a warning glitter—until the door opened, and Roseanne stepped through looking fresh and beautiful—and then he looked at her, as did every other man present. Including Marcel. She couldn't blame him; beside the sparkling Roseanne, she felt dull and uninteresting. Not wishing to keep Marcel from joining the others round the Portuguese girl, Kate walked across to the bar to get another unwanted drink.

She could have joined the noisy group; they would have accepted her into their circle, made her feel welcome, but perversely she didn't want to join them—she wanted them to join her. Or for Adriao to—but he quite obviously didn't want to.

As she topped up her glass with orange juice, her glass was taken from her hand. 'It won't help, you know,' Adriao said softly in her ear. 'Neither will trying to make me jealous by chatting up Marcel.'

'I wasn't chatting him up,' she denied stiffly. 'Neither was I trying to make you jealous. Why should I?'

'Because you are unsure of yourself, of me, of what I want from you. Because you're frightened——'

'Frightened?' she scoffed.

'Yes, little Kate, frightened of putting yourself in someone else's power. Frightened of not being in control.'

'Nonsense! And hadn't you better get back to Roseanne? I think she's calling you.' As he automatically turned to look, she picked up her drink and slipped away. Walking across to one of the long sofas, she sat down. Leaning back, she closed her eyes and tried to shut them all out. She wanted to go to her room that she supposed someone had organised for her—and sulk, Kate? she asked herself.

With a long sigh, she opened her eyes and stared down into her drink, then looked round in surprise as Roseanne came to sit beside her.

'Hello, you are Kate, are you not?' she asked with a friendly smile. 'You must be exhausted, and that wretch Adriao is neglecting you.'

'Well, I expect he'd rather talk to his friends,' Kate said lamely, perversely now wanting to champion him. 'Can I get you a drink?'

'No,' she denied gently. 'Are you hating me very much, Kate?'

'Hating you?' she asked cautiously. If Adriao had been telling her of her reaction...

'Yes, I would be hating you if you had thrown yourself into Mandel's arms, if you had turned up at the reception looking freshly pressed and made up and I was all grubby and crumpled from a long drive...'

Looking down at her creased trousers and shirt, she sighed, then looked up with a wan smile. 'Yes, I'm sorry. I was hating you, because I'm stupid, because I'm tired, because I've been thinking things that probably aren't true. Because I'm being maudlin and paranoid; because I feel dull and crumpled—and because——'

'And because she is in love with me and won't admit it,' Adriao put in softly from above her head.

Flinging her head up in shock, she looked awkwardly up at him, her eyes wide, frightened almost.

'And because,' he continued gently, taking the seat that Roseanne hastily vacated, 'my attempts at psychology have sadly failed again.'

'Is that why you've been ignoring me?'

'Mmm—after such a promising start in the service station when for the first time you actually touched me of your own volition, I was hoping you would make the first move.'

'The first move?'

'Yes, up till now, I've been making all the running.'

'Running?'

With a slow smile, he smoothed back an errant strand of hair from her bewildered face with a gentle finger. 'Yes, Kate, running. What did you think I'd been doing?'

'Tormenting me?' she whispered, her eyes fixed widely on his.

'And why do you think I've been doing that?'

'To make me mad? To confuse me?'

'To draw you out, to make you admit to something you're resolutely determined to deny. So now tell me honestly how you feel.'

'Tired, confused, hurt—and wanting,' she finally admitted, her voice low and husky, barely audible.

'Yes, and wanting,' he agreed with soft satisfaction. 'As I have been wanting—very badly.' Curving one palm round her neck, he drew her face to his, his eyes on hers.

With a little shiver of awareness, she moved her eyes to his slightly parted mouth and felt her breath catch.

'Wanting,' he murmured, his breath feathering across her lips, 'and probably too tired to relieve it.'

With a little snatched breath, she closed her eyes as his mouth touched hers, then expelled it raggedly as he drew back and blew softly on her eyelids.

'Ready for bed, my darling?' When she gave a jerky little nod, he removed the glass from her hand, helped her to her feet and escorted her from the room. Kate carefully kept her eyes lowered, not wanting to see anyone else's reaction to their departure.

Taking a key from his pocket, he opened her door and ushered her inside, then, picking her up, he lay her gently on one of the beds and lay beside her. His eyes holding hers, he gently touched his fingers to her temple, her jaw, then trailed them slowly across her breast, down to her waist then straightened her rumpled clothing as though it were important she wasn't disarranged in any way. Returning his hand to her waist he exerted gentle pressure to draw her closer, his mouth meeting and touching hers, moving, adjusting, parting, until she was pliant and melting, her body aching with need.

Moving his head back a fraction, he ran his tongue across her parted lips and Kate slowly opened her eyes.

'Nice?' he asked softly.

Swallowing the lump in her throat, she nodded.

'So say it.'

'It was nice,' she whispered huskily.

With a little smile, his eyes amused, he picked up one of her hands and held it to his mouth. 'Only nice, Kate?'

'No.'

'No, not something you can describe, is it? So when are you going to marry me?'

'Marry you?'

'Yes, marry me, and you will really have to do something about this deplorable habit of echoing everything I say.'

With a faint smile, she asked sleepily, 'Why do you want to marry me?'

'Because I love you,' he explained simply, and Kate watched his mouth as though that might make it easier to make sense of his words. 'As you love me, don't you?'

'Yes.'

'Yes.' Gently moving her head into the angle of his shoulder, he pulled the bedcover up over the side and across her, then did the same his side so that they were cocooned like a double chrysalis.

'Adriao?' she asked sleepily. 'Did you love Candida?'

'No, Kate. I told you, it was arranged. Now close your eyes and go to sleep. We have five hours before we have to attend the celebratory lunch.'

Tired, slightly bewildered, warm, and feeling somehow safe, she closed her eyes and within seconds was fast asleep.

The midday sun shining full on to her face woke her and she stared in bewilderment at the unfamiliar room until memory rushed back. She was still curled warmly against Adriao and she carefully turned her head to examine his face for a few moments. Close enough to touch, his long lashes hiding his eyes, his thoughts. His mouth slightly parted and she felt warmth flood her stomach, an aching need to press her mouth to his, touch her fingers to his face, and suddenly, unexpectedly, he opened his eyes, and smiled.

'Hello,' he murmured softly.

'Hello.'

'We have a lot to talk about today, a lot of things to do, things we won't hurry. So, we will get up, shower, dress, go to the reception, pretend that we are ecstatic that Vitor has won. We will clap politely and then when everyone else has gone, and we are left in peace, we will come back here, and talk. Yes?'

'Yes,' she whispered.

With a gentle, almost chaste kiss, he unwound them from the bedcover and got to his feet. Looking down at his crumpled clothes with a rueful smile, he sat to tug on his shoes.

'I will come for you in half an hour?'

'Yes.'

With a little nod, he picked up his own room key from the dresser where he had left it and walked quietly out, closing the door softly behind him.

Staring wide-eyed at the closed door, her thoughts in turmoil, she touched a hesitant hand to her mouth. He hadn't been exactly ardent, had he? Just a gentle kiss. And earlier he'd merely bade her go to sleep. Yet he'd said he loved her. Wanted to marry her. A cautious acceptance in her eyes, she scrambled from the bed and went into the bathroom to shower.

When Adriao returned for her, his hair still damp, his chin freshly shaved, she was dressed in her sadly creased dress that she had forgotten to take out of her holdall, but her hair was dried and brushed into a fluffy halo, her face glowing, her amethyst eyes brilliant.

With a smile, he bent and pressed his mouth to hers, and she was a little comforted to see that his grey trousers and pale blue shirt were as crumpled as her dress. Taking her hand, he led her along to the suite where everyone else was already assembled. A long buffet now ran along one wall, and small tables and chairs had been set out. Accepting the glass of port that she was handed, she pinned a smile on her face as the speeches began. The cup was presented to Vitor and Marcel, and she clapped politely, glancing at Adriao as she did so to see if he looked unhappy that he had not won. He didn't. He was smiling along with everyone else. A good loser? Or just a good actor? Then she was cross with herself for her too ready suspicions. He'd said he loved her, wanted to marry her; why on earth couldn't she just accept it? Because it didn't feel quite real?

Mandel, it turned out, had incurred the most penalty points, for speeding—and getting caught— which was apparently what had delayed him, then, at a signal from one of the marshals, the group began to disperse and Kate walked across to the buffet, suddenly finding she was starving, and feeling rather flat.

Turning to smile at Roseanne as the other girl joined her, she loaded her plate from the excellent selection set out.

'Hello, Katherine,' she greeted with a wide, teasing smile, 'you are looking much happier now. You and Adriao have talked?'

'Yes,' she agreed with a hesitant smile for the other girl.

'Good, because I am told I must not speak to you until you had done so!' With a mischevious grin, she added, 'Come, let us sit over there in the window and you can tell me all about it; these men, they just want to talk to each other.'

Collecting a cup of coffee, she followed Roseanne to the small table beneath the window, her face clearly reflecting her puzzlement. Why on earth wasn't Roseanne supposed to talk to her?

'It is all right now, about the money?' Roseanne asked as she munched daintily on a stick of celery.

'Money?' Kate asked in bewilderment.

'*Sim*, the money he needs for the beach site. Of course Mandel and his friends will loan it to him if you do not wish to do so, there is no problem for that, but as you are so wealthy a lady...' She grinned, her eyes twinkling with humour. Seeming not to notice Kate's blank expression, she continued blithely, 'Always these things come at the wrong moment, *sim*? Money needing to be raised quickly, Adriao over-committed on another project... So many business projects has Adriao.' She laughed as though it was all too amusing.

'Yes,' Kate murmured lamely. Not wishing the other girl to see her ignorance, but desperately needing to know what she was talking about, she wondered how to phrase her questions, but Roseanne didn't need any prompting.

'Always it is the same,' she added in happy ignorance. 'Don't you also find it so? When one thing it goes wrong, everything it goes wrong. That is why he wanted you to drive, no?'

'No,' Kate denied blankly. 'Peter had chicken-pox——'

Laughing delightedly, Roseanne exclaimed, 'He hasn't told you? What a wretch he is! There was nothing wrong with Peter! It is a big joke!'

'Joke?' she echoed weakly. Staring at the vivacious face opposite, Kate had a sudden vivid recollection of that evening on the terrace when Carlos had made his dramatic entrance, her suspicion that Adriao was amused, that both men were behaving oddly. 'There wasn't anything wrong with Peter?' she asked slowly.

'No!'

No, she thought, her brows drawn into a heavy frown. That was why he and Carlos had been trying to keep her away from the other drivers in Porto. Because they all knew the truth. 'Everyone else knew, didn't they?'

'Of course!'

'Because Adriao told them?'

'No! Marcel! Adriao was very cross, it was very funny. I will explain,' she added kindly when Kate continued to look puzzled. 'Vitor, of course, knew because it was he who had to pretend to take Peter to the airport with this so very fictional illness, so of a necessity Peter has to tell him the truth. He swore him to secrecy and stayed instead with Vitor at his home. Unfortunately, Marcel, he see Peter in Porto the day before the race and the dog was very firmly from the bag.'

'Cat,' Kate corrected automatically. 'And Marcel told everyone?'

'Yes! That is why I was laughing so much in Santander,' Roseanne went on. 'Marcel had just told me of the joke and I was telling Adriao how naughty he was.'

'I see.' Old friends, she thought bleakly. Old, loyal, secretive friends who all stuck together and thought it was amusing that she was being conned. So that was why he had needed her in the race, not for all the reasons she'd put forward, but because he wanted her to lend him money. Just like everyone else, wanting her only for what she had, not for herself.

Lowering her eyes to the table, a small cold hard lump inside of her, she pushed her plate to one side, and then suddenly remembered something Carlos had said, about why Adriao had been bad-tempered that day. Business problems. Money problems? And it had been about then, hadn't it, that Adriao had started being nice to her?

'You would like something else instead, Kate?' Roseanne asked. 'Me, I could not eat that if you pay me.'

'No, no, it's all right, I'm not really very hungry,' she mumbled. Picking up her cup and holding it between her palms as though she needed the warmth, she sipped at her coffee, her eyes still lowered, her thoughts racing as she tried to remember back to her stay in the *castelo*. Both Adriao and Carlos had insisted she stay there, hadn't they? There had been Carlos's casual questions about her work. Adriao's jibes about her wealth. And his insistence on her being in the race was because he needed her money and that would be a good opportunity to ask her. Did that explain the talk they were to have? Not about their future, but about a loan? Over-zealous, Carlos had said he was, and when she'd teased him, he'd looked annoyed and walked away... Suddenly aware that Roseanne was staring at her in puzzlement, she forced a smile.

'We haven't discussed the details yet. I expect we'll talk about it later.'

'Yes, of course, when we have all gone and you can be in peace,' she agreed, unconsciously echoing Adriao's own words. 'I was so angry with myself in Santander, that I might have spoiled it all. But I did not know he had not yet told you, and me so impulsive to kiss him. I wanted to come after you, explain, when I saw how hurt you were, but Adriao said, no, he would do so. He did?'

'Yes.' He'd said that Roseanne had kissed her husband too. And that he and Mandel were rivals. And he hadn't wanted her to talk to her, had he? Roseanne had already admitted that, which had to be true, because earlier, when the other girl had come to sit beside her, Adriao had very quickly abandoned his friends and joined her, hastily breaking in on their conversation. One minute he'd been indifferent, and the next, all loving...

'For long time I have known Adriao, and Mandel of course,' Roseanne continued, happily oblivious of Kate's troubled thoughts. 'We were all childhood friends. They vie for me like silly boys.' She laughed. 'But I have choosed Mandel—and now Adriao has choosed you.'

'Yes. Adriao has choosed me. The wealthy Kate Lassiter.'

'But of course. It is nice to have money, no?'

'Oh, yes, it is nice to have money,' she echoed bitterly.

'I have said something I should not?' Roseanne asked worriedly, her brows drawn into a frown. 'My English is sometimes not good, the words sometimes wrong. But do you not have here that the old, wealthy families marry to each other?'

'Sometimes, except that I'm not from an old, wealthy family—it's not important. Tell me, do you love Mandel?'

'Love?' she asked, almost as though Kate had said an unfamiliar word. 'He is my husband.'

'Yes, but do you love him?' Kate insisted.

'We are compatible, we laugh together, we hope to have children together,' she explained in an obvious desire to be helpful, but she was clearly puzzled by Kate's words.

'The marriage was arranged?'

'Of course.'

Of course. 'Did you consider marrying Adriao at one time?' she asked quietly.

'But yes, Adriao is of an old, revered family. My parents must consider him.'

'But you chose Mandel.'

'Yes, because Adriao always he is so busy doing this, that.' She laughed. 'Building projects, tourism—me, I am bored by these things. I think it would be nice to have big, smart hotels for Portugal, but Adriao, he busies himself here and there to stop it. He only wishes to buy the beach site to stop the developers. What use will he have for it? An empty piece of land? Now he must sell shares in this and that for the money—or did. Now it will be all right, of course.'

'Of course.' Because he met the stupid and gullible Kate Lassiter. Who is so very wealthy. 'Did you know Candida?' she asked bluntly, not even really sure why she did so.

'But yes, Candida I had known from small child. We all did. She was very foolish——'

'Not hungry, Kate?' Adriao asked, suddenly materialising beside her, but, without waiting for her to comment, he grinned at Roseanne. 'And what dark secrets have you been imparting to my intended wife?' he asked jokingly.

'No, I have not told Kate any of your past indiscretions,' she said, laughing back. 'Shall I?'

'No.' He grinned.

'Very well, then I will not. No, Kate and I have been talking about her lending you the money for the beach site. She has not known very much about it, so I have been explaining——' Then she broke off with a bewildered, hurt look as Adriao said something in his own language. Something angry and almost savage-sounding.

Turning to look up at Adriao, she saw his face was set, cold, as he continued to speak rapidly to Roseanne.

With a little cry of distress, the other girl got to her feet, glanced once at Kate, her face stricken, then back to Adriao, her lovely eyes filling with tears. As she tried to turn away, Adriao caught her arm, pulled her towards him, and spoke softly, rapidly and Roseanne nodded. Giving Adriao a watery smile, she said something softly to him, then went quickly to stand by her husband, who gave her a curious glance before looking across to Adriao and Kate.

Placing her cup shakily back in her saucer, Kate tried to get to her feet, her face averted, knowing she wouldn't be able to cope with a showdown with Adriao at that moment, and certainly not in front of all his friends who would not understand. Did none of them marry for love? she wondered bleakly.

'Kate?' Adriao said quietly.

'No,' she gasped as she fought to hang on to her control and push her chair back and escape. Only he was in the way and she couldn't move. With something very like a sob, she struggled frantically until Adriao wrenched the chair aside and caught her arm. When she tried to twist away, he took a firmer grip and, keeping his bulk between her and the rest of the room, he urged her towards the door. Thrusting her through it, he propelled her along the corridor to his own room and pushed her inside, then stood with his back against the door.

'No running away, Kate, not this time. What did Roseanne say? Come on,' he instructed quietly. 'Say it all.'

Whirling to face him, her body stiff and straight, her hands clenched by her sides, she stared at him, her eyes very bright. His face was the bland, quiet mask that she had once been used to, his eyes giving nothing away of his thoughts. But he was angry, she knew he was angry, very, very angry. Well, he would be, wouldn't he? All his little plans thwarted.

'If you had asked,' she said coldly, her voice shaking with the effort to keep it steady, 'I would have lent you the money. There was no need for this charade.'

'Go on,' he said quietly.

'What do you mean, go on?' she demanded. 'What more is there to say? Except that I'm stupid.' Turning away from him, she began to pace back and forwards, her feelings in turmoil. 'You had me on a nice piece of string, didn't you, Adriao? One tug, and like the fool I am I stumbled towards you. What was the next move? An engagement? I lend you the money, you buy your piece of land, and then we find we aren't compatible? Is that it? That's the criterion, isn't it?'

she asked bitterly, turning to face him once again. 'Compatibility? An ability to laugh together? Have children together? Roseanne was quite astonished when I asked her if she loved Mandel! Yet no one would have blamed you when the engagement was broken off, would they? Ah, they would say, poor little English girl, didn't understand the rules! Well, you knew I didn't understand the rules, didn't you?' she yelled, her voice breaking. 'Why? Why in God's name couldn't you just have been honest? Or wasn't I worth even that? And Peter! I thought he was my friend! Do you have any idea how much that hurts? That he could set me up like that? That you all could? You promised me you did not lie! That day in your study—and it was all a pretence!'

'Was it?' he asked coldly.

'Yes! A ruse!'

'Carlos's ruse, not mine. I do not indulge in ruses.'

'Then what the hell do you call chicken-pox?' she screamed. 'The truth?'

'No, it was, as I thought, a harmless deception cooked up by Peter and my uncle. They knew of my wish to be alone with you, they thought the race would be a good opportunity.'

'Oh, and it was, wasn't it?' she demanded tearfully. 'Only it all nearly came to grief, didn't it, when Roseanne threw herself into your arms and you kissed her so passionately!'

'I kissed her so passionately, as you put it,' he enunciated in his cold, precise voice, 'in a desire to protect you. Knowing of your trouble with the Press, your dislike of notoriety, I hoped it might take the attention of the photographers away from you, allow you to get to the hotel unmolested. Which it did.'

'And you expect me to believe that? She told me, Adriao! Told me you were sharing a joke! At my expense! Oh, get out of here!' Swinging away, she slammed her hand into the wall, her shoulders heaving in dry sobs.

Walking across the room, he turned her round and captured both her hands in his. 'Have you finished?' he asked, his voice still quiet, his face blank. When she didn't answer, just glared at him, her lovely eyes filled with tears, her breath coming still in jerky little sobs, he continued levelly, '*She* was sharing a joke. Not I. Roseanne is used to being courted, fêted, admired; it would not occur to her that my motives for kissing her would be different from her own. And I most certainly had no intention of explaining them to her,' he added distastefully. 'Everything else she said to you was true, except in one respect. One very important respect. By her own reading of things, by her own upbringing, way of life, it was all as she understood it. I needed money quickly. A loan, to buy a piece of land that a developer also wanted, to build a hotel on. I did not want him to build a hotel. The building committee had decided not to stop him. So I did. *Did*, Kate, not will, not can, but did. I have already raised the money, which will be repaid when I have realised some of my assets. I do not discuss my business dealings with anyone, not Carlos, and certainly not Mandel or his wife. Mandel knew I was trying to raise cash because his brother is manager of my bank—which will no longer be my bank if the manager cannot desist from discussing my affairs!' he added with quiet savagery. 'Mandel offered me a loan—he is quite wealthy. I declined. He knew you were staying at my home—he knew you were wealthy because he also knows Peter and Isabella and something had obviously been said. But not by me. He also added two and two—and came up with five. In a small community such as ours, where everyone knows everyone else, affairs are discussed, dissected, interpretations put forward. It is quite usual in my country to marry for money. They interpreted the facts to suit themselves, and, because I refused to discuss them, answer their questions, and because in Roseanne's world women do as they are told, believe what they are told, she assumed I had an arrangement with you. Which I do—*did*,' he corrected with slight bitterness, 'but not for your money. I do not want your money. I have never wanted your money—and, even if I had been desperate, which I wasn't, I would never have asked you. And,' he continued, his face darkening, 'if my business affairs had been such that I was unable to support my own lifestyle, I would never have asked you to marry me. You think I have so little pride, Kate? That I would ask a woman to support me? Is that what you think of me? Or that I would deliberately hurt a woman? Cheat her? Lie to her?' Dropping her hands, he stepped back. 'Now you may go,' he concluded flatly.

Staring at him uncertainly, at his cold arrogant face, the pride that tautened the skin across his high cheek-bones, she knew he hadn't lied. Knew he never would—he was, as he had said, far too proud. With a little shuddery breath, knowing she had thrown it all away, she practically ran to the door and escaped along to her own room. Hurrying inside, she leaned back against it, her breathing snatched and jerky, her tears spilling over to run down her face. She could still hear the talk and the laughter from the reception-room along the corridor and wondered if Adriao had rejoined them. If his mask was back in place.

He'd said he loved her, and, perhaps, in his own way, he did. Had, she corrected with another shudder. Had. She doubted a man with his pride would be able to forgive her for not believing him. Yet she didn't think he could love her as she did him. Not with passion, or any sort of desperate feeling. He'd kissed her more passionately in his study before he'd professed to care for her. Why? Yet it no longer mattered why, did it? Her own insecurity, feelings of inadequacy, had made her throw it all away. Wiping her palms across her wet cheeks, she moved towards the bed. Sinking down on the edge, her face in her hands, she began to cry again, then looked up quickly, defensively, as the door opened.

Staring at Adriao as he stood framed in the entrance before coming in and closing the door quietly behind him, she swallowed hard. Did the gods allow second chances?

Her tear-washed eyes fixed widely on his face, she got to her feet. Holding her hands tight in front of her to steady their trembling, she took a deep, shuddery breath and whispered almost inaudibly, 'I'm sorry.' When he remained silent, his dark eyes expressionless, she hurried on, 'I shouldn't have believed her.'

'Then why did you?'

'Because I didn't think you could love me—no one else ever has,' she admitted thickly as her eyes filled once more with tears.

'Oh, Kate,' he exclaimed on an escaping breath. 'Oh, Kate.' Reaching forward, he pulled her into his arms and held her tight, her face pressed into his neck.

Winding her arms round his waist she hugged him to her as though she would never let go, sniffing frantically to halt fresh tears. 'Please don't be angry with me any more,' she husked thickly. 'It sounded so plausible and it all seemed to fit. It seemed that you only began being nice to me after Carlos had mentioned your business problems, and then the race and everything, you kissing Roseanne, Peter not being ill . . .'

'Easier to believe all that, than that I love you?' he asked gently, easing her away to look down into her woebegone face.

'Yes. I'm not a very lovable person. I'm aggressive, defensive, I shout at people, lose my temper——'

'Get all scrambled up?' he teased softly.

'Yes.'

'You also devote your time to old people, young children, you're loyal and tough, a fighter—and under that tough exterior is a frightened baby, a little girl who nobody loves, hmm?'

'Yes. My mother disliked me; my father; a boy I was in love with when I was eighteen admitted he only wanted me because of the money. He told me I was plain and stupid and should count myself lucky that someone was prepared to marry me.'

'Poor Kate,' he taunted with a gentle smile. 'And you believed him?'

'Yes—no,' she denied shakily, 'I knew it was only sour grapes because he'd thought I would be an easy touch, and I wasn't. But the words sort of stayed inside, so I suppose I half believed them.'

'And was determined that never again would anyone pull the wool over your eyes. So you never let anyone get close, attacked first before they could do so.'

'I suppose so.'

'And do you suppose that all those men who tried to get close to you only wanted you for your money?

Not for your beautiful eyes? Your smile? You have a beautiful smile, my Kate. A beautiful nose—a beautiful mouth,' he added softly, his eyes lowering to examine it. 'And I love you very much.'

Parting her mouth with exquisite tenderness, he kissed her with slow enjoyment, then lifted his head and smiled down at her. 'So, you will marry me, yes? And come to live in my castle?'

'Yes,' she whispered.

'And you will not mind that Carlos will also be there?'

'No.'

'And you will be able to set up your centre without running it yourself?'

'Yes.'

'And you will not mind leaving your old people and your children?'

'No.'

'Good. We have old people and children in Portugal,' he said gently. 'If you should wish to work, it is up to you. But hopefully you will be too busy caring for me and our own children.'

'Yes.' Yet he still didn't kiss her with passion and she raised a troubled face to him again. 'Adriao? When we were in your study and you—wanted me, you kissed me as though...'

'Ah, as though I would not be able to stop, and you are wondering why I am now so restrained. Yes?'

'Yes,' she whispered. Lowering her eyes from the bright intentness of his, she traced one finger round a button on his shirt, then gave a little start when he tilted her head up.

'Look at me, Kate.' When she had raised her eyes to his, he explained quietly, 'I thought you would understand. Your eyes, and your attitude, were asking

for time, pleading with me not to rush you. You were
so unsure of yourself, of me, of my feelings, I didn't
want to frighten you.'

'Is that why you didn't tell me about Peter?'

'*Sim*. If I told you, and you refused to drive, I was
no further advanced, was I? I did not find it amusing,
Kate, to keep steering you away from Marcel, who is
quite incapable of keeping his mouth closed.'

'I thought you were jealous,' she whispered.

'I was. You think I like to see an attractive
Frenchman kissing you?'

'If Peter had driven, you might have won.'

'And lost you?' he asked gently. 'Oh, Katie, so dis-
trustful, so on the defensive.' Trailing a gentle finger
down her cheek, he added softly, 'You sometimes look
as though you've been hurt so many times, are so defeated and angry, that I want, oh, I don't know, to
do something stupidly quixotic, I expect. Only you
never want sympathy, or pity, you just want to have
a fight with someone.'

'Yes,' she agreed, because it was true. 'I thought
Peter—oh, Adriao, I couldn't bear it thinking that
you had both set me up.'

'Hush,' he soothed gently.

'He has been my friend for such a long time. It
explains why Isabella was so amused, though, doesn't
it?' she asked, a faint smile in her eyes.

'Yes, she thought it hysterical. So did Carlos, but
then he has always thought the pair of us hysterical,
which was why he added a few little touches of his
own, like Eleanor, like inviting her round that evening,
like telling you I was going to marry her.'

'Is that why you were so angry that night?'

'No, that was because you shoved me away in the
garden, as though you found my touch distasteful.'

'But you didn't—want me then,' she said carefully.

'I didn't know I wanted you then,' he corrected with a faint smile. 'I do now. I want to kiss you, make love to you, very much, but you are an innocent, yes? I do not want to shock you, frighten you.'

'You won't,' she whispered softly. Then, raising her face, she gave a little chuckle. 'I don't think I'll be shocked, but you might be. I have a horrible feeling that I will be very wanton.'

'Horrible?' he queried humorously, yet his voice sounded thick, husky. 'I don't think I could find anything about you horrible.'

'You did once.'

'No,' he denied, 'just confusing.'

'And argumentative...'

Smiling, he shook his head. 'No, I suspect that's what attracted me in the first place. I discovered in myself a desire to fight with you, bait you. Reprehensible, hmm?'

'Shocking. So why did you insist I stay at the *castelo*?'

'I don't know. I never quite understood it myself. A whim? An unacknowledged desire to get to know you better?'

'You could get to know me better now,' she prompted daringly.

'Yes,' he agreed thickly.

'So will you? Make love to me? Kiss me properly?'

His eyes darkening, he framed her face with palms that shook slightly, then, with a muffled word in his own language, he picked her up and carried her to the bed. 'Yes, Kate, I will kiss you properly—and perhaps I will not be able to stop.'

'I don't want you to stop,' she whispered shakily, her voice husky and uneven, and, just before his mouth lowered to hers, she asked unsteadily, 'Adriao? What was it you were going to tell me at the service station in France?'

With a slow smile, he admitted, 'Why, to tell you that I loved you, of course.'

'Of course,' she echoed as his mouth claimed hers.

# HARLEQUIN
## *Romance*®

and WEDDINGS go together—
especially in June!
So don't miss next month's title in

# THE BRIDAL COLLECTION

### LOVE YOUR ENEMY
### by Ellen James

**THE BRIDE** led the anti-Jarrett forces.
**THE GROOM** was Jarrett!
**THE WEDDING?** An Attraction of Opposites!

Available this month in
THE BRIDAL COLLECTION

### THE MAN YOU'LL MARRY
### by Debbie Macomber
Harlequin Romance (#3196)
Wherever Harlequin books are sold.

WED-2

# Harlequin Presents®

## Coming Next Month

Available in June wherever paperback books are sold, or through Harlequin Reader Service:

In the U.S.
P.O. Box 1397
Buffalo, NY
14240-1397

In Canada
P.O. Box 603
Fort Erie, Ontario
L2A 5X3

# ® *Harlequin* ®

# JANELLE TAYLOR

# *Valley* of *Fire*

**HARLEQUIN IS PROUD TO PRESENT *VALLEY OF FIRE* BY JANELLE TAYLOR—AUTHOR OF TWENTY-TWO BOOKS, INCLUDING SIX *NEW YORK TIMES* BESTSELLERS**

VALLEY OF FIRE—the warm and passionate story of Kathy Alexander, a famous romance author, and Steven Winngate, entrepreneur and owner of the magazine that intended to expose the real Kathy "Brandy" Alexander to her fans.

Don't miss VALLEY OF FIRE, available in May.

---

## "GET AWAY FROM IT ALL" SWEEPSTAKES

# HERE'S HOW THE SWEEPSTAKES WORKS

### NO PURCHASE NECESSARY

To enter each drawing, complete the appropriate Official Entry Form or a 3" by 5" index card by hand-printing your name, address and phone number and the trip destination that the entry is being submitted for (i.e., Caneel Bay, Canyon Ranch or London and the English Countryside) and mailing it to: Get Away From It All Sweepstakes, P.O. Box 1397, Buffalo, New York 14269-1397.

No responsibility is assumed for lost, late or misdirected mail. Entries must be sent separately with first class postage affixed, and be received by: 4/15/92 for the Caneel Bay Vacation Drawing, 5/15/92 for the Canyon Ranch Vacation Drawing and 6/15/92 for the London and the English Countryside Vacation Drawing. Sweepstakes is open to residents of the U.S. (except Puerto Rico) and Canada, 21 years of age or older as of 5/31/92.

For complete rules send a self-addressed, stamped (WA residents need not affix return postage) envelope to: Get Away From It All Sweepstakes, P.O. Box 4892, Blair, NE 68009.

© 1992 HARLEQUIN ENTERPRISES LTD.                    SWP-RLS

---

## "GET AWAY FROM IT ALL" SWEEPSTAKES

# HERE'S HOW THE SWEEPSTAKES WORKS

### NO PURCHASE NECESSARY

To enter each drawing, complete the appropriate Official Entry Form or a 3" by 5" index card by hand-printing your name, address and phone number and the trip destination that the entry is being submitted for (i.e., Caneel Bay, Canyon Ranch or London and the English Countryside) and mailing it to: Get Away From It All Sweepstakes, P.O. Box 1397, Buffalo, New York 14269-1397.

No responsibility is assumed for lost, late or misdirected mail. Entries must be sent separately with first class postage affixed, and be received by: 4/15/92 for the Caneel Bay Vacation Drawing, 5/15/92 for the Canyon Ranch Vacation Drawing and 6/15/92 for the London and the English Countryside Vacation Drawing. Sweepstakes is open to residents of the U.S. (except Puerto Rico) and Canada, 21 years of age or older as of 5/31/92.

For complete rules send a self-addressed, stamped (WA residents need not affix return postage) envelope to: Get Away From It All Sweepstakes, P.O. Box 4892, Blair, NE 68009.

© 1992 HARLEQUIN ENTERPRISES LTD.                    SWP-RLS

## "GET AWAY FROM IT ALL"

### Brand-new Subscribers-Only Sweepstakes

## OFFICIAL ENTRY FORM

This entry must be received by: April 15, 1992
This month's winner will be notified by: April 30, 1992
Trip must be taken between: May 31, 1992—May 31, 1993

**YES,** I want to win the Caneel Bay Plantation vacation for two. I understand the prize includes round-trip airfare and the two additional prizes revealed in the BONUS PRIZES insert.

Name _____

Address _____

City _____

State/Prov. _____ Zip/Postal Code _____

Daytime phone number _____
(Area Code)

Return entries with invoice in envelope provided. Each book in this shipment has two entry coupons — and the more coupons you enter, the better your chances of winning!
© 1992 HARLEQUIN ENTERPRISES LTD.                    1M-CPN